One Bed for Christmas

Baldwin Village, Book 0.5

Jackie Lau

First edition: December 2018

Print ISBN: 978-1-989610-40-4

Edited by Latoya C. Smith, LCS Literary Services

Cover by Jay Pillerva

Author's Note

One Bed for Christmas can be read as a standalone romance, but it's also a prequel novella for my Baldwin Village series.

Baldwin Village is a real place in downtown Toronto, east of Chinatown and Kensington Market. It's a small section of Baldwin Street where the houses have been converted to a diverse set of restaurants, shops, and cafés, many with nice patios out front.

This series revolves around a fictionalized version of Baldwin Village—all of the businesses are of my own creation. It's meant to feel like a multicultural village within a big city.

The first novel, *The Ultimate Pi Day Party*, focuses on a pie shop, Happy as Pie, which is mentioned in this novella.

Prologue

Wes

Twelve years ago...

IT'S ONLY THE THIRD day of class, and I've already missed one lecture.

I should have been in physics two hours ago, but I didn't wake up when my alarm went off, and now that I'm living away from home, there's no one to yell at me when I dare to sleep past eight.

There's also no one to stop me from playing foosball until two in the morning. Funny how that happened.

I hurry across campus and jerk open the door to the building where I have calculus. I'm a couple minutes late, but I'm determined to make it and maybe even take notes. I'm in my first year of computer engineering at Waterloo, and I should at least make a bit of an effort.

My knapsack slung over my shoulder, I hurry toward the lecture hall that's just over—

Shit. I'm going the wrong way. As I said, it's only the third day of class, and I still don't know what I'm doing. Clearly.

Okay, the lecture hall is in sight. Almost there.

I'm reaching for the door handle when all of a sudden there's a blow to my head and I fall, hitting my head again on the floor.

Blearily, I open one eye. I must have been out for a few seconds.

And then I open my other eye so I can get a proper look at the sight before me.

"Oh my God," the Asian girl leaning over me says. "Oh my God. I'm so sorry. I didn't mean to smack you in the head when I opened the door."

I know her. There aren't a lot of girls in my class, and she's the one who wears shirts with actual buttons and sits in the front row and occasionally asks intelligent questions. She's the kind of girl who wouldn't sleep through her physics lecture and wouldn't be running late to calculus...although it appears that's what she was doing today, like me.

She's also gorgeous, I realize now. In fact, I rather like lying on the floor outside the door to my calculus class, one hand pressed to the bump forming on my head, if it means I get to look at her. She has long, shiny black hair, dark eyes, and really awesome lips. I don't know what makes them so awesome—I just got hit in the head twice, after all—but I think they would be really great lips to kiss. She's wearing a short-sleeved white shirt (with buttons, of course), a teal vest, and a headband.

Suddenly, I find headbands extraordinarily sexy.

"Are you okay?" she asks, and to my surprise, she pulls out a goddamn first aid kit from her knapsack. Who carries a first aid kit to class?

I kind of love it, though.

She presses a hand to my forehead, and *oh my God*. I groan because it feels so good when she touches me.

This girl, however, seems to think my groan is a sign that I'm in terrible pain. I suppose I haven't actually spoken yet, and she worries I have a serious head injury.

I'm not thinking clearly, but it's not because I hit my head.

"What's your name?" she asks.

"Wes."

"I'm Caitlin."

And that's how I fell in love with Caitlin Ng.

Chapter 1

Caitlin

It's eight thirty on a Saturday night, and I'm at the office.

I know, I know, I'm pathetic.

Not only is it a Saturday night, but it's the Saturday before Christmas, which is on Tuesday. I don't have anything planned for Christmas, though. My parents are spending the holidays in Hong Kong, and I have no siblings, no other family in Canada. Mom wanted me to go with them, but the idea of spending two weeks away from my company gave me heart palpitations.

Sometimes it's still hard to believe that this is my life: I'm the CEO of Match Me, one of the most popular dating apps in the world. I worry that one day, I will open my eyes at five in the morning, and it'll all be gone, everything that I've worked so hard for.

I continue to work as hard as I can. Hence, I'm at the office on a Saturday night before Christmas, but I'm finally ready to head back to my house in Cabbagetown, and no, I will not do any more work tonight. I will heat up some food, make some hot chocolate, and maybe even watch a movie.

See? I can have fun. It might not involve any socializing, but it's fun.

I peek out the window to see what the weather is like and jolt back in surprise.

There must be twenty centimeters of snow on the ground. There was only a sprinkling when I was out at lunch, and now there's been a ton of accumulation. The snow is still falling, the wind blowing it sideways.

I check my phone, and sure enough, everyone is talking about the snowstorm in Toronto, which is supposed to continue until tomorrow afternoon. Somehow I was so caught up in my work that I missed the news.

No big deal. I'll hop on the subway, take it to Wellesley, and walk from the station. It'll be a bit slow-going, but I'll manage. Then I'll curl up with my dinner and hot chocolate, safe from the storm.

My phone beeps. It's a message from Claudette, my neighbor. She's a retired paleontology professor who enjoys baking cookies and talking about the Cambrian explosion.

The power's been out on our street for an hour. I don't expect it'll be back on anytime soon. Just letting you know, in case you're still at the office.

I go to the Toronto Hydro website and look at the outage map. There are power outages everywhere, and I suspect Claudette is right—it'll be out for a while. In the 2013 ice storm, I was without power for days.

The thought of braving the weather, only to return to a lonely home with no heat and power, makes me shiver. That sounds horrible.

What else can I do? I could try to get a hotel room, but that's equally unappealing. On the Saturday before Christmas, it seems beyond pathetic.

I've been alone all day, and suddenly, I really don't want to be alone anymore. I guess I could go over to Claudette's, and we'd talk about Mary Anning and Christmas cookie recipes (not that I bake) in the dark.

Or is there someone I could stay with nearby? Who do I know who lives downtown and *doesn't* work at my company?

I tap my fingers on my executive desk as I think.

Wes Cheng! I haven't seen him in a few months—my social life is rather limited—but I think he still has an apartment near Baldwin Village. Less than a ten-minute walk from my office on Dundas, or maybe fifteen with all the snow on the sidewalk.

I send him a text, and a few minutes later, I receive a response. *No problem. I'm at Prince & Pauper Pub right now. Meet me there?*

Of course Wes is at a pub. It's a Saturday night. We're in the midst of a snowstorm, but still. Wes isn't the sort of guy to stay at home on a Saturday.

I slip off my shoes and put on my big winter boots, down jacket, scarf, and toque, ready to brave the cold.

It is indeed cold outside. Well below freezing and the wind stings my bare cheeks. I push my scarf up to my nose and wrap my arms around myself. Thankfully Prince & Pauper is only a few minutes away.

I'm about to open the door to the pub when I'm knocked to the ground. When I look up, there's a T-Rex standing above me.

I scream. This is, I believe, the natural reaction when one finds oneself on the ground, staring up at an enormous T-Rex.

Although...aren't T-Rexes supposed to be even bigger than this? Plus, they've been extinct for sixty-five million years.

Right. It's not a real T-Rex, just someone wearing a ridiculous inflatable T-Rex costume.

But then the T-Rex speaks. "Caitlin."

Oh my God, how does it know my name?

There's only one likely explanation: the T-Rex is Wes.

"Sorry for scaring you," he says, his voice muffled by the costume. I can see part of his face through the clear panel in the T-Rex's neck. "Guess I finally paid you back for knocking me out in calculus class."

My cheeks heat at the memory, even though I'm half-lying on a snow-covered sidewalk.

The first time I met Wes was back in university when, in a hurry to get to a calculus lecture because somehow I'd lost track of time while studying at the library (yes, really), I opened the door and smacked him in the face. I hadn't seen him, as I was so focused on getting to class on time. I was never late, and I prided myself on that fact.

Instead, I ended up knocking out a guy, and the entire lecture hall turned to look at us as I frantically tried to get him to speak and reassure me that I hadn't done any real damage. He didn't say anything when I asked if he was okay, just stared at me. Finally, I got him to tell me his name.

That's how I met Wes Cheng. He forgave me, and we became friends. Stayed friends after university.

And now, it's the first time I've seen him in months, and he's dressed as a T-Rex. Something that would be terribly out of character for me, but not so much for him.

Although it's still pretty weird.

Wes tries to bend down to help me up, but he can't quite manage it in his costume.

I start laughing. I can't help it. "I'm fine, don't worry about it."

"Sometimes I forget how big this costume is."

I'm about to ask why he's dressed as a dinosaur—Santa Claus would be more appropriate, given the time of year—when an elderly white man pokes his head out from behind the door. "Wes, we're back on in five."

I get to my feet. "Wait a second. You're performing in a T-Rex costume?"

"Yep," Wes says. "I'm a dancer."

"A stripper?"

"Why are you assuming that I'm going to strip off this lovely inflatable T-Rex suit, Caitlin? Something in particular you'd like to see?"

Oh my God. My cheeks heat again. I'm not used to Wes talking to me like this. Nor am I used to talking to a person wearing an inflatable T-Rex costume.

"Come on," he says, struggling to open the door. "You can see the show."

I head inside, no idea what to expect, and get a Coke. Unfortunately, the pub is packed so I have to stand, and since I'm pretty short, I don't have a great view. Wes in his T-Rex suit should still be easy to spot, though, but he's nowhere in sight.

Instead, four elderly men walk onto the make-shift stage and start singing "Silent Night" a cappella.

Okay, I'm confused. What does Wes have to do with a barbershop quartet?

Laughter ripples through the room. The T-Rex is making his way onto the stage, wearing a poinsettia garland around his neck. He turns around, his back to the audience, and shakes his tail, and there's even more laughter, but all the singers keep a straight face.

None of this makes any sense whatsoever.

I haven't laughed so much in a long time.

One of the older men hands a drum and a drumstick to Wes. They sing "The Little Drummer Boy," Wes beating along on the drum and dancing energetically.

Next, another of the singers puts a swaddled doll into Wes's T-Rex hands, with a big sign that says "BABY JESUS." A few seconds later, they start singing "Away in a Manger," and Wes rocks the doll throughout the entire song.

When the song is over, one of the singers places a set of angel wings on Wes's back. They sing "Angels We Have Heard on High" while Wes dances, completely out of time with the music, and occasionally roars. This is followed by "Jingle Bells" and "O Holy Night," after which the lead singer announces that there will be only one more song.

The audience lets out a collective "Aww" and the quartet begins singing "Winter Wonderland." Wes dances along, and halfway through, someone in a snowman suit does two shots and joins him on stage. As they hold hands and start dancing together, I experience an unexpected moment of jealousy, wishing I was the snowman.

Not that I've ever wanted to dance in front of an audience in a snowman costume before, but knowing Wes, I bet he's having a lot of fun right now.

Fun is not something I've been very familiar with lately, but despite the snowstorm and power outage at my house, tonight has turned out okay.

Chapter 2

Wes

WE WALK BACK TO my apartment, Caitlin in her sensible down jacket and me in my T-Rex costume. It turns out that walking around in an inflatable T-Rex costume during a snowstorm is rather difficult, and I wish I'd brought my jacket with me.

"Did you enjoy the show?" I ask Caitlin, even though I know she enjoyed it very much. I was watching her throughout most of it.

"I did." She cracks a grin, then sobers. "I'm sorry. I've been so busy and we haven't spoken in ages...and then I turn up, asking to stay with you right before Christmas."

"It's no problem." I wave this away.

When the only woman you've ever loved needs your help, you don't say no, even if you've been avoiding her lately.

The reason for keeping my distance? I figured I finally needed to make an effort to get over Caitlin, after more than twelve years of being pathetically in love with her. I want to stay friends, but I thought a little time apart would do me good.

It hasn't worked the way I'd hoped, though. I still love her.

It's not like anything will ever happen between us. From the first week of school, when I saw Caitlin sitting in the front row and studiously taking notes—and when she knocked me to the ground—I knew she was going places, and I wasn't.

Sure enough, she graduated at the top of our class, and I'm lucky I graduated at all.

Still, it's a degree, a degree in a challenging program at a prestigious university, but I discovered along the way that I had no interest in engineering or anything related.

Now I'm a freelance graphic designer, and I also make extra money here and there from random gigs, like the one I did tonight.

And she's a goddamn CEO.

I'm happy with my life now, but I still feel like she's a little too good for me, though that feeling has faded somewhat with time. I'm okay with who I am.

But she's never shown any interest, and it's apparent I'm not her type. She dates successful guys who are good at wearing suits and yelling on their phones, and I...well, I can make her laugh, and I can be there when she needs me.

I stumble through the snow in my costume. Caitlin grabs my arm when I nearly topple over.

"I have to ask," she says. "How did you become a dancing T-Rex for a barbershop quartet?"

"I saw an ad on a lamppost. Bernie, the bass, got the idea from a real estate listing. Some photos of the property included a T-Rex, and it went viral. He figured that might be a clever way to get attention for their barbershop quartet, which has been together since the seventies. He was tired of doing the nursing-home circuit and wanted to book some bigger venues for Christmas. Five people auditioned, and I was the best," I say proudly. "My performance during 'The Little Drummer Boy' apparently put me over the top."

Seriously, these T-Rex costumes are an awesome invention. Whoever thought of them is a genius.

Have you ever seen a picture of someone wearing an inflatable T-Rex costume and not, at the very least, cracked a small smile? Many months ago, I came across a photo of someone wearing a T-Rex costume and walking a dog, and it made my day.

That's why I usually walk home after these performances in my costume. The streets aren't busy tonight, but people are pointing at me and laughing—in a good way. It brings them joy. It fits right in with the Christmas spirit.

A group of drunk young men ask me for a picture. I growl in response, and just as they're about to head away, I gesture to Caitlin and say she can take the picture.

As we climb the stairs to the third floor of the small apartment building I live in, I'm huffing and puffing with the difficulty of manoeuvring in this costume. Finally, we get inside, and Caitlin helps me strip.

Alas, helping someone strip out of a dinosaur costume isn't exactly sexy.

Caitlin, however, looks so freaking cute in that matching toque and scarf. Her cheeks are flushed pink, and her lips look so...kissable.

Which was exactly what I thought the day we met and she knocked me on my ass.

I didn't mean to do the same to her. I just figured I'd meet her out on the street and surprise her, plus the costume is pretty warm, despite the fan, and I needed to cool off.

Instead, I knocked her over, but she laughed and got up without any difficulty.

I would never want to hurt her.

I know Caitlin can be hurt, even if she comes across as an invincible woman who can handle anything life throws at her.

She takes off her winter garments and hangs them up. Underneath, she's wearing a soft brown turtleneck and dark jeans, and yeah, she's pretty cute. She's even wearing a headband today, which she doesn't do often anymore, but that was her trademark back in university.

She looks around my apartment—she's never been here before—and I try to see it through her eyes. My heart sinks.

My place isn't a complete dump, but it's an old, poorly maintained building, and although I'm not a slob, I'm not as neat as I could be.

I don't see any disappointment flicker across her face, though.

"My bedroom's just through that door." I point. "I'll sleep on the futon."

"Oh," she says quietly. "*Oh.* You only have one bed."

She must have assumed I'd have a guest room. Ha. No way am I paying for a two-bedroom apartment in this ridiculous rental market. But being a CEO who owns a detached house, she would have things like guest rooms.

"I'm sorry," I say. "I know it's not what you're used to."

"It's fine! I can't ask you to give up your bed. I'll sleep on the futon, don't worry."

I'm not going to let her do that, but I table the argument for now. "Have you had dinner?"

"Oh, shit! No, I haven't."

Well, we can't have that. I ate at the pub, but I have a nice pulled pork pie in the fridge, which I was planning to eat for lunch tomorrow. I got it from the pie shop, Happy as

Pie, down the street. Caitlin can have that instead of me. I know she loves pie of all kinds, and I'm glad I can provide her with one.

I take out a bag of spinach from the fridge and make her a salad to go along with the pie. She tries to help me, but I shoo her away.

A minute later, she's hooked up her phone to my crappy speaker system and "All I Want for Christmas Is You" fills my apartment.

Oh, man.

If only she knew.

But I've always hidden my desire for her. Even joking about anything related—like what I said earlier when she asked if I was a stripper—is out of character.

I use the bag of spinach as a microphone and goofily sing along, snapping my fingers as I dance around the kitchen. Caitlin giggles, like I knew she would, but then she does something I didn't expect.

She picks up the salt shaker and starts singing with me.

I've never heard her sing before, and it's soon obvious why: Caitlin Ng is good at almost everything, but she can't sing worth a damn.

Still, it's endearing; it's rather perfectly imperfect.

She's also swinging her hips and her boobs are jiggling a little, and I'm certainly not complaining about the show.

We sing the entire song together, pointing at each other every time we say "you." When it's over, we're both flushed and laughing, and I bend down to slide the pie into the pre-heated oven before returning my attention to the salad.

It's a perfect moment of domestic bliss, singing unselfconsciously in my kitchen and preparing a late dinner for the only woman I've ever wanted to be my own.

But I need to be careful. I'm supposed to be finally getting over Caitlin, not falling for her even more.

Chapter 3

Caitlin

WHEN I TEXTED WES and asked if he'd put me up for the night, I didn't think about the fact that he wouldn't have a guest room. Why would he? And as far as one-bedroom apartments go, his is pretty small. He doesn't have space for a guest.

I should have gone to a hotel, but I know Wes won't let me go out in the snowstorm now.

Actually, I enjoy being in his apartment, away from the mountain of work I have. I don't feel like Caitlin Ng, who, by some fluke, became a successful CEO. I'm just a woman, letting loose a little.

God, I can't believe I sang in front of him. I only sing in the shower. When it's someone's birthday, I mouth the words because I am acutely aware that I suck at singing. I was great at piano, but my voice is horrendous.

Wes doesn't care though, and I always liked that about him. He doesn't care what anyone thinks, and he doesn't worry.

I'm a bit of a worrier. Always have been. In university, my solution was to overstudy, so I knew the material cold. But Wes cheerfully walked into our electronic circuits exam saying he had no idea what a circuit was—an exaggeration of course—and that he was sure he was going to fail.

I always admired how he could do that.

For the record, he did pass the course. Barely.

Now he's preparing me a salad and meat pie, and it's kind of sweet.

"I'm glad you were free tonight," I say. "It occurred to me that you might be, well…"

Oh, God. I'm mortified that I was thinking about this.

"Santa Baby" comes on. I don't know why I put this song on my phone. I've always hated it.

Wes sings along in an exaggerated voice. He struts across the kitchen, then stops in front of me. "It occurred to you that I might…what, exactly?"

"Have a woman over," I stammer. "A woman you intended to, well, bang."

Yeah, I sure have a great vocabulary.

He chuckles before turning away from me and going back to the salad. "Right."

I always admired that about Wes, too. How easy it is for him to approach a woman and charm her. How he could have casual sex, just let go for a night.

All of the sex I've had has been confined to relationships, and I haven't had one of those in well over a year. Ironic, perhaps, considering I run Match Me. Many people have found love because of my app, yet my love life is non-existent.

And if you're wondering if Wes and I have ever hooked up, the answer is no.

I've never thought of him in that way.

I look at him now, singing along to "Santa Baby" as he whisks up a vinaigrette. He certainly does have a cute smile, and adorably untamable hair, and broad shoulders, and nice arms.

Come to think of it, Wes is pretty good-looking, and it's no surprise that he's often successful picking up women at the bar. Not that he does it when I'm around, but I've heard stories.

Hmm. He's handsome, and he's currently cooking me dinner...

But no. Wes is my friend, and I'm sure he's never thought of me in that way before, either. I mean, the first time I met him, I smacked him in the face, and I'm far too much of a nerd for him.

We get along great as friends, but I can't see us being anything else. We're too different, and honestly, the fact that this is the first time I've even thought about the possibility, despite knowing him for twelve years, should mean something.

Wes doesn't seem interested in relationships anyway. I've never known him to have a girlfriend for more than a month, and even that is a rare occurrence.

He walks over to the oven and takes out the pie. It smells amazing.

"For you." He puts it in front of me with a flourish.

"Want some?" I gesture to all the food. I feel guilty—I'm about to stuff my face, and he's not eating anything.

He shakes his head. "I ate earlier, but you know what? I think I'll have some hot chocolate. And under no circumstances will I make any for you. Nope, won't even consider it."

"Wes..."

"Okay, fine. If you sing 'Santa Baby' for me."

He's joking. Wes knows better than to deprive me of hot chocolate. I love hot chocolate, preferably with lots of marshmallows on top. He, on the other hand, likes his with a shot of Bailey's.

I know I don't have to sing "Santa Baby" to get hot chocolate, and I know my singing voice is absolute shit, and oh my God, I really do hate that song, but for some reason—to catch him off guard, I guess—I stand up and grab the salt shaker again. Wes widens his eyes, and then he grabs a Santa hat off the top of the fridge (why does he have a Santa hat on top of the fridge?) and puts it on. He sits down, hands behind his head, smirking.

"And now," he says, "we have a special guest. Caitlin Ng, CEO of Match Me, will perform her rendition of 'Santa Baby.' Please give her a warm welcome!" He claps his hands and starts the music.

I just stand there.

As a CEO, I have to do a lot of things that many people find nerve-racking. That *I* still find nerve-racking. Like making enormous decisions, speaking in front of large groups, and firing people.

And I do it all. Sometimes I need to talk myself up a bit first, but I know I can do it.

This, however, is a different story.

"Santa Baby" is a sexy song, and Wes is an attractive guy and my friend, and my voice is utter crap, and I've never been good at embarrassing myself in public.

Yet a part of me wants to prove to him that I can be more than nerdy and driven, and singing "All I Want for Christmas Is You" was kind of fun, much to my surprise.

Still, I can't find it in me to make this big a fool of myself.

"You know what will make you feel more comfortable?" Wes says. "An inflatable T-Rex suit. It's like a mask. It's easy to do anything when you're wearing a T-Rex costume, and everything you do can't help but be awesome."

And this is how I find myself being helped into an inflatable T-Rex costume at eleven in the evening on the Saturday before Christmas. I dance and sing along to the song in a not-so-sexy way, while Wes howls in laughter and takes a video that better not end up on social media.

Finally, I remove the costume and sit down in front of my salad and pie. I'm grinning and flushed. It's nice to hang out with Wes, after being so anti-social for the past several months. It's nice to not be worried about what everyone thinks.

Alright, no matter how long the power outage lasts and how long I end up staying with Wes, I resolve to not even think about Match Me until after Christmas.

Three days with no work. The thought is overwhelming, but I'm determined to succeed.

I need more balance in my life.

I need to hang out with Wes more than once every four months.

It's midnight, and I'm down to my last sip of hot chocolate. Despite the hot beverage, and despite all the moving around I've done, I'm getting a bit chilly. When I shiver, Wes gets up and puts his hand on the radiator.

"Heat's gone off," he says.

"The heat is off?" I squeak. "Can you turn it back on?"

"Nah, I have no control over it. Something must have broken again. Happens occasionally. The super will get to it eventually."

"Eventually?"

"Hopefully tomorrow or Monday."

"Tomorrow or Monday?"

I know I sound like an idiot.

But no heat? That's why I came to Wes's. He was supposed to have functioning electricity and heat. Maybe I sound like a princess, but I'm already chilled, and it's only going to get worse.

Wes doesn't sound too bothered by it, but unlike me, he probably doesn't run cold.

He gets an extra blanket for the bed and gives me a pair of sweatpants and an ugly Rudolph sweater. Rudolph has a large red pom-pom for a nose, and I sort of love it.

"Are you sure you're okay with sleeping on the futon?" I ask.

He nods. "You take the bed. I'll be fine out here."

He's wearing pajama pants and a white T-shirt that does great things for his arms.

Hmm. I really shouldn't be noticing such things about my friend.

Because that's what Wes is. A friend who's kind enough to let me stay the night, make me dinner, sing "All I Want for Christmas Is You" with me, and lend me his T-Rex costume.

He's not going to give me a kiss goodnight.

OMG, Caitlin, where did that come from? Why are you thinking about kisses?

Perhaps because I haven't so much as kissed a guy in over a year and my body is desperate. Yeah, that must be it.

Maybe I'll get Wes to teach me his secrets to picking up and casual hook-ups. God knows I'm not any good at those things, but right now, as I survey the double bed and the wind howls outside, a hot male bed partner sounds pretty appealing.

Alright. I'll put that on my New Year's resolutions list. *14. Get laid.*

Yes, I've already got the first thirteen resolutions figured out. I keep a running list in a New Year's resolutions app on my phone, which also helps you track your progress.

I look forward to tracking my progress for this one.

But tonight, I'm alone.

Ah, well.

It's now two in the morning, and I still haven't fallen asleep.

It's fucking freezing. How can his apartment get so cold when the heat has only been off for a few hours?

I'm also finding it rather lonely in here, even though I'm used to sleeping alone in my bed, alone in a house that I have all to myself.

Wes, on the other hand, is probably soundly asleep on the futon, his bigger body providing enough heat to keep him warm.

Sharing a bed with my male friend sounds a little strange, yes, but you know what?

I really am very cold.

I leave the bed and head to the living room.

Chapter 4

Wes

Here's the thing about my futon.

I got it at a deep discount and soon discovered why: it's the least comfortable futon known to mankind. Like, seriously, it's an impressive feat that anyone managed to make such an uncomfortable futon.

It's not a bad place to lounge—with lots of pillows—while you're watching a movie, but it's a terrible place to sleep.

I mean to replace it eventually, but I keep spending my money on other things. Recently, I've spent a lot on Christmas preparations. I don't usually go all out like this for Christmas, but this year is a little different in my family, and I am determined to bring a ridiculous amount of Christmas cheer to my parents' house on Monday.

I roll onto my stomach, but the futon is even more uncomfortable in this position. How is that possible?

Ugh. I don't know what time it is now, but it's going to be a long, long night.

If only I could be with Caitlin instead. But offering her the full use of the bed was the right thing to do. There's no way I'd let her sleep on this travesty of a futon, and I couldn't expect her to share a bed with me. Plus, that would give my body ideas.

"Wes."

It sounds like Caitlin, but I must be imagining it. The pain of sleeping on this futon must be making me hallucinate. It can't actually be her.

A small hand—a very cold small hand—covers my mouth.

"Sorry!" She jolts back. "I was aiming for your shoulder, but I couldn't see in the dark."

I exhale. "What's up? Is something wrong?"

"I'm cold."

"I'm sorry I don't have any heat, not even a space heater." I want everything to be perfect for Caitlin, but alas, I cannot control the whims of the silly old building I live in. "I'll get you another blanket and a pair of fuzzy socks."

"That sounds excellent, but I was actually wondering if you'd like to join me in bed?"

I couldn't have heard that right. Maybe I'm hallucinating after all.

I flick on the lamp. Caitlin really is here, sitting on the edge of the futon.

"Are you propositioning me?" I ask.

I cannot tell you how many times I've dreamed of Caitlin inviting me to her bed. Or my bed, in this case.

She's wearing one of my ugly Christmas sweaters, and her normally neat hair is a mess, but she's still the most beautiful woman ever.

I've thought that since I was an eighteen-year-old kid.

Since she was the studious girl in my class who sat in the front row, and I was the goof in the back row. Since before she started conquering the world.

I always knew she'd succeed.

"No, no," she says hastily, and I can't help but deflate. At least she doesn't sound disgusted by the possibility. "I just thought...well...the bed is probably more comfortable than this futon. I hate imposing on you like this, but..."

This hesitancy isn't like her.

"I thought we could snuggle for warmth," she finally says.

"You thought we could snuggle," I repeat stupidly. "For warmth."

"Yeah." She balls her hands up in my enormous sweater. "I'm so cold I can't sleep."

"And you want me to share my body heat with you."

"Yes, and I'll share mine, too. If I have any, that is."

I stare at her, wide-eyed.

Caitlin wants to fall asleep in my arms. It's not like she wants anything more than to steal my body heat, but still.

This is dangerous. Really fucking dangerous. This won't help me get over her.

"If you don't want to," she begins, "it's okay. I know it's awkward, since we're not, you know." She gestures between us. "But I thought..."

"It's no problem," I say, telling myself I'm just being a good friend.

Uh-huh.

In the bedroom, I get Caitlin a pair of fuzzy socks that I was given for Christmas one year. They're too warm, so I never wear them, but that's exactly what she needs.

Then we climb into bed together and I turn off the light.

God, this is surreal.

"So, uh, how are we going to do this?" she asks. "I'll be the little spoon?"

"Yes, that works." My voice is a bit rough.

She curls up on her side, hands under her head, and I curl myself around her, my chest pressed to her back. I don't know how I'm going to sleep tonight, because this just feels so damn amazing and I want to treasure every minute of it.

I'm very sappy when it comes to Caitlin Ng. Always have been. In fact, I'm an absolute pile of marshmallow goo when it comes to her, and she feels as good in my arms as I'd dreamed she would. She fits against me just perfectly.

But in addition to having mushy thoughts about her right now, I'm also having sexual thoughts. I can't help it, especially not when she shimmies and rubs her backside against me as she gets comfortable, obviously having no idea what she's doing to me. I ache to feel her bare skin against mine.

However, I have twelve long years of practice in hiding my attraction to her. This is nothing I can't handle, right?

"Better?" I ask.

I'm met with a cute little snore.

Yes, even her snores are lovely.

When I wake up the next morning, I'm surprised to discover that last night was not a dream. Caitlin and I are still in bed together, and are, in fact, still snuggling.

I spent an utterly chaste night with her—well, chaste everywhere except my mind—and I can't help hoping her power isn't back on yet. I can't help hoping she'll stay with me.

I have lots of things to do this weekend. In addition to decorating my tree, I plan to spend lots of time in the kitchen. The two of us can do it all together and, once again, be the perfect picture of domestic bliss.

I check the clock. It's eight o'clock, and I suspect Caitlin is usually at the office by now. But not today. Today she's...

"Oh. *Oh*."

...making some sexy noises in my bed. Is she having a sex dream? Does it involve me? (Probably not.) How often does this happen?

She turns onto her other side so we're face-to-face and wriggles her hips against me.

I already had morning wood. Is morning stone a thing?

Time to get out of bed, and maybe I should stop hoping her power is still out. Spending a day with Caitlin is really fucking dangerous for me.

Oh my God, now she's hooking her left leg over my hip?

I let out an unsteady breath, and then I carefully put her leg back on the bed and get up, even though I desperately want to stay.

In the kitchen, I decide to make pancakes for breakfast, and I've just poured the first batch into the pan when Caitlin emerges from my bedroom, wearing my ugly Rudolph sweater, my sweatpants, and my fuzzy socks. Super cute.

"I can't believe I slept in until after eight," she says with a yawn.

"When do you usually wake up?"

"Five or five thirty."

About what I'd expected. I, on the other hand, usually wake up about now. One of the perks of working from home. At first I was terrible at it, seeing as I'm not the most disciplined person, but I soon got the hang of it. I had to.

"You're making pancakes!" Caitlin claps her hands with childlike excitement, and I smile. "I haven't had pancakes in ages."

As I hand her a mug of coffee, I can't help but think about those breathy noises she made in bed. I'm too distracted to say anything, but luckily, she doesn't notice.

She takes a seat at the table. "My power's still out."

I'm glad she's letting me cook for her, rather than insisting on flipping the pancakes herself, and I can't help a discreet fist pump at the comment about her power.

"Plus, due to the snowstorm, everyone is advised not to leave home," she says, "unless absolutely necessary. It's really bad out there. I wonder if the mayor will call in the army for snow removal, and Toronto will be the laughingstock of Canada again. Anyway, we're basically snowbound together."

I tell my body not to get too excited. "Do you have work to do?"

"Nope, the only thing I'm doing until after Christmas is checking to see if I have any emergency emails. Other than that, I'm free!" She gets up to do a little twirl, then sits back down. "I really need a break but have no idea what to do with myself. What are your plans for today?"

"Making orange pomander balls, shortbread cookies, and hopefully a gingerbread house from scratch."

"Wow, that's ambitious!"

I can't help but feel a little twinge. "Yeah, it's totally out of character for the guy who didn't even try to pass signals and systems the first time around and was more concerned with the foosball tournament on campus."

"Hey!" Caitlin says. "It's almost Christmas. Why all the negative talk? Besides, you just weren't in the right program, but you felt obligated to tough it out because of your parents. You're hardly lazy and stupid. You know that, right?"

I step away from the stove to grab the maple syrup out of the fridge. "Yeah, I know."

It was definitely the wrong program for me, but I still feel a little guilty that I did such a piss-poor job in school and wasn't able to stand up to my parents until after it was all over.

But Caitlin doesn't think I'm lazy, and her opinion matters to me.

I set a plate of pancakes in front of her, and she gives me an enormous grin, which I can't help but return.

· ♥ · ♥ · ♥ · ♥ · ♥ ·

Caitlin and I are kicking ass at preparing for the holidays. It's noon and there's an entire bowl of orange and clove pomanders on the table, a batch of shortbread cookies cooling on a rack, and we're in the middle of assembling the gingerbread house.

Caitlin hasn't questioned my desire to go all-out for Christmas, and she didn't ask for an explanation when I dumped a bag of ten oranges on the table and started pricking them with toothpicks. I made the designs with the toothpicks, and she pushed in the cloves after I was done. We made a good team.

Now, however, I think our streak of success is coming to an end.

My plans for the gingerbread house are very elaborate. It's supposed to be a two-story house with a second-floor balcony, a chimney, a door, and eight windows with shutters. We've also baked several trees, plus a sleigh and two reindeer to go on the roof.

I've never made a gingerbread house before, but I was sure it would be no trouble, despite all the baking disasters I saw while binge-watching *Nailed It!* last week.

Unfortunately, even though we carefully followed my plans and baked all the pieces we needed, the house is now tilting precariously to the right, and I have yet to install the chimney.

I assemble the four sides of the chimney, pipe some royal icing onto the sloping roof, and place it on top.

I back away, hands in the air.

The chimney slides off the roof and onto a gingerbread tree, which crashes to the table.

"I told you there was a problem with the structural integrity of the house," Caitlin says. "We should have made a triangular-prism gingerbread house. Fewer pieces. No balcony, no chimney."

"Who lives in a triangular prism house?" I say. "Nobody."

"Uh, what about these people?" She shoves her phone in my face. She's done an image search, and her phone now displays a series of houses that are, indeed, perfect triangular prisms.

"If you look hard enough, you can find anything," I grumble, "but a triangular prism house looks like a tent to me. I want to make a *proper* house."

"The fact that the house is made of gingerbread is already a serious knock against it being a *proper* house."

"Wouldn't living in a house of gingerbread be fun? You could eat the walls."

"Which would destabilize the house and the roof would come crashing down. You'd have some serious structural integrity problems."

"Look at you, talking like an engineer."

"We do both have engineering degrees."

"In computer engineering, not structural engineering."

I enjoy bickering with Caitlin. I've missed it in the past few months. It's all in good fun, and I can't help but imagine ending one of these arguments with a kiss. Can't help but imagine toppling onto the lumpy futon and tearing off her clothes.

I shake my head, trying to clear it of that thought.

"Okay, okay." I rake my hands through my hair. "We won't have a chimney. Or maybe we'll have a two-dimensional chimney rather than a proper four-sided one, and I can put the sleigh and reindeer on the front lawn rather than on the roof."

"Very sensible." Caitlin reaches out to...

Oh my God, she really is going to touch me.

"You have royal icing and sprinkles in your hair," she says. "Tip: don't run your hands through your hair when you're making a gingerbread house."

I exhale slowly as she removes the icing and whatever else I've got in there.

When she finishes, she doesn't immediately step back. We stand there for a moment, much closer than friends normally stand. I want to pull her against me and share my body heat with her—the heat still hasn't come back on, and she's been wearing her toque inside all day. I want to lick icing off her finger, feed her the remaining three sides of the gingerbread chimney, and make her moan like she did in her sleep. Having those noises in my mind is torture.

Instead, I take a step back and say what a man always says when he's lusting after a woman he can't have.

"How about we start on the gumdrop forest?"

I'm pretty sure it's just my imagination, but I swear I see a flicker of disappointment cross her face.

Chapter 5

Caitlin

THERE'S SOMETHING INCONGRUOUS ABOUT sitting in a hipster bar, surrounded by men sporting man-buns and flannel, and watching as a barbershop quartet—all of them wearing suits and straight faces—sing "Once in Royal David's City" while a man in an inflatable T-Rex costume does the floss dance.

It makes zero sense, and it's kind of wonderful.

I'm at a table off to the side, having a great time even though I'm not drinking. I rarely drink because I'm one of the many East Asians who suffers from Asian glow. I turn bright pink and get slightly nauseous when I consume alcohol, but more concerning to me is that drinking when you have Asian glow damages your DNA and leads to an increased risk of esophageal cancer, and I'm not taking any chances.

Hence, I usually avoid alcohol. Plus I don't like how my brain gets fuzzy when I drink, either. I don't like the sensation of losing control.

Though I felt like I was losing control earlier today.

Wes cooked me breakfast, which made me warm and fuzzy inside. I can't remember the last time anyone took care of me like that. None of my exes ever cooked me breakfast.

And then seeing him with icing and candy in his hair...well, that was kind of adorable, and as I combed the icing out with my fingers, the thoughts of adorableness went out of my head and were replaced with awareness of how close we were. Awareness of how he was bigger and taller and stronger than me, but so safe and caring at the same time.

I nearly kissed him.

We've known each other for twelve years, and I'd never wanted to kiss Wes before, but I wanted to do it this afternoon, when we were working on that disaster of a gingerbread house.

Just a fleeting feeling. I shouldn't think much of it.

With some effort and creativity, we managed to salvage the gingerbread house. It's not as impressive as the ambitious plans Wes had drawn up, but it's still pretty good. I'm rather proud of my gumdrop decorations, and the reindeer look great.

Now, for the second night in a row, I'm watching him dance to "Jingle Bells" as though he doesn't have a care, or a self-conscious bone, in his body.

The T-Rex costume helps you let loose—I certainly felt its effect when I put it on last night—but it's just the way Wes is, too. He's the perfect person to spend a few days with when I'm taking a break from work.

Once the performance is over, we head back to his apartment. The snow has stopped falling, and the sidewalks have been partially cleared, so it's easier than yesterday. The city is no longer strongly advising everyone to stay indoors, which is why Wes still had his performance tonight.

My power, however, hasn't come back on. Claudette last texted me at six o'clock.

Wes's apartment doesn't have heat either, but at least it has electricity, and it has Wes and his ample supply of body heat.

I suspect we'll snuggle again for warmth.

Just for warmth. Not because we have any feelings, sexual or otherwise, for each other. The kiss that didn't happen? That was just a momentary misfire of my brain.

But damn, I really need to get laid. That's probably why I nearly kissed Wes. My body has been deprived for so long.

So later that night, when we're sitting around his kitchen table with mugs of hot chocolate and marshmallows once more, I ask him a question.

"You have lots of sex, right?"

He nearly spits hot chocolate all over me.

"Sex. Me. Lots?" he sputters.

"You sleep around, don't you? I'm not judging. I'm hoping you can teach me."

"Teach you," he repeats. "What, exactly, do you want me to teach you?"

"I don't know." I didn't think this through. "I just…I don't know how to go about having casual sex, but I want to. Women have needs, you know, and I…"

Oh, God. I can feel my face turning red, as red as it turns when I have a couple of glasses of wine. Why did I think it was a good idea to talk to Wes about this? He's my friend, yes, but he's a male friend.

For some reason, I am very aware of the fact that he is male right now.

"You going to Eugene's New Year's Eve party this year?" I ask. Eugene was one of our classmates at Waterloo. "I think that might be a good place to, you know, meet someone? But I don't know how? To go about the whole sex thing, I mean?"

Wes rests his elbows on the table and puts his head in his hands. As though I'm hopeless and he just doesn't know what to do with me.

But I really want to do this. My last few relationships haven't been satisfying, so I don't want to bother with a relationship. Just sex.

"Match Me," he croaks at last. "Are you forgetting that you run a dating site, which caters to people looking for a variety of things, not just long-term relationships?"

"Not happening. People would notice, and it would be weird."

"You're a CEO, you can do whatever you want."

"A female CEO, and people are much more judgmental when it comes to women, plus I expect I'd get trolled a lot. I can't use Match Me like a normal person. So back to this party...how should I act?"

"Assuming there's a guy you want to bang."

"A guy I want to bang. Yes."

I'm uncomfortable with this conversation, but that's to be expected. However, I didn't expect Wes to look so uncomfortable. He's usually laidback and easygoing, not fazed by anything.

"Well, you should, uh, flirt with him."

"I don't know how to flirt."

"Sure you do. Maybe lean in close, casually touch him."

I brush my hand over Wes's shoulder.

"Or you could just do what you did last night in bed."

I freeze, my hand still on his shoulder. "What did I do?"

He grins and has a long sip of hot chocolate, then goes to pull something out of the fridge. "Bernie's wife made fruitcake. You want some? I've never actually had fruitcake before."

I don't say anything.

"I hear it's the least popular Christmas gift," he continues, "and some people think it should just be used as a doorstop. But we'll see, won't we?"

"Wes..."

"A large slice, is that what you're saying?" He cuts two pieces, places them on a plate, then returns to the table and takes a bite. "Not bad."

"Wes, what did I do last night?"

"Oh, nothing. You just stayed sweetly snuggled up beside me the whole night."

I'm frantic. Somehow it's very important that I know what happened, and Wes isn't helping. So I grab the deflated T-Rex costume from the floor, as well as a fork.

"Tell me or I stab the costume and it won't inflate anymore."

"You should see your face right now." He pries the costume and fork out of my hands. "I'll tell you, don't worry. I just enjoy riling you up every now and then."

I give him a dark look.

"There were some noises," he says, before raising the pitch of his voice. "Oh, oh, *oh*. Then you turned to face me and wiggled your hips against me, and you hooked one leg over my hip. That's when I got out of bed to make pancakes and let you have your sex dream in peace."

"I didn't have a sex dream!" I sputter.

"Mm. I think you did. Pity you don't remember it."

"I'm so sorry, Wes. I didn't realize I did that in my sleep. I guess that's what happens when you never share a bed with someone—you have no one to tell you these things."

I'm mortified. Not only did I ask my friend to snuggle for warmth, but I tried to hump him while I was asleep!

It's still cold in here, but I suddenly feel rather warm.

"Don't apologize," he says. "It's fine. I didn't mind."

"You didn't mind?"

"Well, it was sort of awkward, but there's no need to apologize. It's not like I've never thought of you in that way."

"Right. Because straight guys always think about having sex with their female friends?"

"I only do that with you."

He's looking at me with an intensity I rarely see on his face. I feel pinned to my chair.

I'm waiting for him to kiss me.

I'm waiting for *Wes Cheng* to kiss me.

I stuff some fruitcake in my mouth, and to my horror, start talking while I'm chewing. But I need to ruin this moment. It's probably all in my imagination anyway.

"So where were we?" I ask. "Right. Since I'm not going to put those moves on a guy at a party, what do you suggest instead? And what should I wear to this party if I want to pick someone up?"

"You're beautiful no matter what you wear."

"Don't give me that line."

"It's not a line."

"It's definitely a line. Is that what you use to get women into your bed?"

"Caitlin..."

"Should I try to pick up a guy by telling him he's beautiful no matter what he wears? Even if he's wearing an inflatable T-Rex costume?"

I swallow hard after I say those words. Because as I stare at Wes, who's wearing a plain navy V-neck sweater, I realize something.

He's not just good-looking. No, he's pretty freaking hot, whether he's looking at me intensely like he is now, or stabbing oranges with cloves, or wearing an apron while baking shortbread cookies, or making me laugh.

Okay, I wouldn't say he's especially attractive when he's wearing a T-Rex costume, but you know what? In a way, he kind of is. I love that he does the floss dance while dressed as a Cretaceous carnivore. It's so *him*, and it's funny and charming.

But he's particularly hot when he's sitting close to me, his knees nearly touching mine, and we're all alone in his apartment.

"You really are beautiful no matter what you wear," he murmurs, and then he places his hand on my cheek and strokes it softly.

Oh my God.

I did not know that having one's cheek stroked could feel so amazing.

And this moment...I'm definitely not imagining it.

I lean forward.

He leans forward, too, and he kisses me. When his lips touch mine, it feels good and right, and when he cups my ass, I eagerly move to his lap. I wind my arms around him and increase the pressure; he matches it. Gentle, yet firm, and right now, it's everything. God, I haven't had a kiss like this in a long time.

You're kissing your friend, Caitlin!

Suddenly he sits back, as though he heard my thoughts. He looks embarrassed that he kissed me like that.

"Want to watch a Christmas movie?" he asks.

We end up watching *Elf*, because I think it's the greatest Christmas movie of all time, and we do snuggle, for practical reasons. The radiator is warm in Wes's apartment now—apparently the heat came back on when we were out at the pub. But it'll take a while for the apartment to warm up to room temperature, so we cozy up while watching the movie, and once again, we spoon in his bed, under a mass of blankets, me wearing his sweatpants and ugly Christmas sweater.

There are no more kisses, though.

An hour after we climb into bed, I'm still awake. I fell asleep immediately when he climbed into bed with me yesterday, but today is a different story.

I can't help thinking about our kiss. About how he told me, with all seriousness, that I'm beautiful, and touched me so tenderly. And apparently I put some moves on him in my sleep, and I can't help thinking about that, either.

I'm pretty sure Wes is still awake. His breath, which I can feel on my neck, is not that of a sleeping man, and when I adjust my position, he groans. I press back against him, and I'm shocked—yet, in a way, not shocked at all—to discover he's hard.

As I release an unsteady breath, I'm filled with want.

He feels so good behind me, and I'm sure he would feel even better inside me.

Really, this is just a sensible solution to my problem of needing to get laid, and I'm all about sensible solutions. Rather than picking up a guy at Eugene's party, why don't I fulfill my need for sex with Wes instead? I don't know how things would go with a stranger I met at a New Year's Eve party, but Wes is right here, and he's my friend and I'm completely safe with him. I know he'll treat me well, and

I'm pretty sure he'd say yes, given what happened earlier tonight.

The kiss, brief though it was, felt great, so it only stands to reason that sex would too, right?

"You awake?" I ask.

"Mm-hmm."

"Want to have sex?"

Chapter 6

Wes

Caitlin propositioning me is the stuff of my dreams.

Last night, when she wanted to join me in bed, she only wanted my body heat. Now, however, she wants more.

Wait a second. My mind must be playing tricks on me. She didn't really say that, did she?

"Did you just say you want to have sex with me?" I ask.

I wish I could see her face, but I can't, not in the darkness of my bedroom.

"I did," she replies, "but don't worry. It's just sex. It doesn't mean anything."

That's precisely the problem.

I *want* it to mean something, unlike with any of the women I've slept with before.

Earlier, I told her she was beautiful. I was this close to confessing my feelings for her, unable to stand how she was talking about picking up a guy at Eugene's New Year's Eve party. However, I put my many years of practice at hiding my feelings to good use, and I managed to keep my mouth shut.

Okay, that's not true.

I managed not to tell her my feelings, but I kissed her, and I did *not* keep my mouth shut when doing that. For so long, I'd dreamed of holding her against me and pressing my lips to hers. In far more romantic scenarios than what ended up happening.

But it was amazing nonetheless.

I love her. If I sleep with her, I want it to mean something; of course I do.

Yet she thinks I want the opposite.

I wish I could tell her everything, confess I've been in love with her since she knocked me to the ground and pulled a first aid kit out of her knapsack. There was something so endearing about that first aid kit, and I have the same feeling in my chest now at the practical note in her voice. She sees us as being friends who have sex—just once, or on an ongoing basis? I'm not sure, but she sees it as a practical solution to, well, being horny.

So sex is on the table, and I think our friendship will survive it, but if I reveal my feelings, everything will get really weird. Although she wants to sleep with me, that doesn't change the fact that I'm not her type when it comes to a relationship.

This is not how I'd dreamed things would happen.

But I'm a weak man. The woman I love wants to have sex with me? I'm going to give her exactly what she wants, even if it's not everything I desire.

I'm going to rock her goddamn world.

Unfortunately, I've gone too long without speaking, and Caitlin thinks I'm not interested.

"Sorry," she says, "forget I ever—"

I cut her off with a kiss.

When my lips meet hers, it's electric. I feel like sparks are flying from my fingertips as I stroke the soft skin of her cheeks and slide my hand down to her neck. I press myself against her and feel her curves against my body, even through all those layers of clothing.

"Let's do this," I say, as though I'm talking about making a gingerbread house, rather than something I've desperately wanted for a dozen years. "I want you naked, but if you're going to get too cold—"

"Naked is good, but we'll have to stay under the blankets."

"I can work with that."

I slide off the Rudolph sweater and toss it to the ground, followed by the long-sleeved T-shirt of mine that she's wearing underneath. Then I turn on the lamp beside the bed, because there's no way I'm having sex with Caitlin in the dark.

She instinctively crosses her arms over her chest.

I'm not used to Vulnerable Caitlin. I'm used to Caitlin taking on the world with her incredible work ethic and intelligence and charm.

"I haven't been in bed with anyone in a long time," she says quietly. "I know you've been with lots of women, and—"

"Not as many as you think. And you should never doubt that I think you're beautiful and sexy, even if I never told you that until tonight." I rake my eyes over her bare chest. Her breasts aren't large, but they're lovely, and her nipples are pebbled right now, whether from the cold or her excitement, I'm not sure. "You're special to me," I say quietly, not sure if I want her to hear. "Like no one else."

I place my hands on her sides and stroke my thumbs up the slope of her breasts and over her nipples. To my satisfaction, she whimpers. Then I set my mouth to one nipple, rolling my tongue over the tip as I stroke her other nipple with my hand, dragging another whimper out of her. Instinctively, she moves her hips up toward me, and I get even harder.

My sweatpants are loose on her, and I easily slip the tips of my fingers inside the waistband, waiting for her nod before I continue further. When she gives it to me, her pretty lips parted, I slide my hand into her panties and draw my middle finger along her slit.

Oh, fuck. She's wet for me.

My cock desperately wants to be inside her, but I also want to give her pleasure before we get there. I want her mindless, begging me to take her. I want her to shatter in my arms. We might only do this once, and I want it all.

I slip my finger inside her, and we both groan.

"Good?" I ask, running my other hand through her hair. She nods.

"You just tell me if there's anything you want, at any time," I say.

"Well, there's one thing…"

"Yes?"

"I was hoping you'd go down on me. You know, if you're into that."

"Of course that's part of my plan. I don't know if I should be offended that you thought you had to ask."

She chuckles, but then I press my finger deeper inside her, and she groans. It sounds just like one of the groans she made in her sleep last night.

I grin and slide my head under the blankets and down between her legs. I pull out my fingers and give her one long, slow lick.

She grabs my hair, holding me down, keeping me where she wants me.

I love it.

In fact, she's gripping my hair tightly enough that there's a bite of pain, but I like that. I circle my tongue around her clit, then over her entrance. She bucks her hips toward my face, and I love that, too. I thrust my fingers inside her again and continue to pleasure her, reveling in the feel and taste of her.

God, she's amazing.

And this is real, utterly real, so much better than all the times I imagined it.

Her breathing becomes jerky, and I grab her ass and press her against my mouth, the better to ravish her. I feel her muscles tense, and then she comes apart in my arms.

I glance up. "How was that?"

In response, she pushes my head back between her legs, and I give her exactly what she wants. She squirms against me, and it's not long before she orgasms again.

As she shakes and shatters and cries out in my arms, I wonder, just for a moment, if maybe I'm enough for her. If I can give her what she needs outside the bedroom, too.

That never seemed like a possibility to me before, but for a flash, it is.

Caitlin is pawing at my shirt, trying to take it off, but her movements are clumsy. I save her the trouble and whip it off myself, and the noise of appreciation she makes is gratifying. She runs her fingers over my pecs and abs as though I'm a work of art, made just for her.

Anything for you, Caitlin.

But I don't reveal any of the feelings that I've kept bottled up inside for so long. Instead, I smirk and say, "See anything you like?"

"I knew you were fit, but I didn't know you looked like *this*."

I take off my pants next, and she stares at the bulge in my boxers. Hungrily.

It's still hard to believe this is actually happening. Tentatively, she reaches inside my underwear and wraps her hand around me. I hiss out a breath.

"You're so...so..."

She can't find the words, and I know what that's like.

Caitlin Ng is touching my cock, and for once, this isn't just a fantasy.

As she slowly slides her hand up and down, I slip my fingers between her legs again and find her soaking wet. It's easy to push three fingers inside her, and she groans once more.

"Wes, please."

"Please, what?"

"Fuck me. I want you to fuck me."

Jesus. I love hearing her talk like this in bed.

I reach into my bedside table for a box of condoms. It's buried under a few other things. Contrary to some people's beliefs, I don't have a different woman in my bed every couple of weeks, and it's been a while since I've used this box.

I rip open the foil packet and roll on the condom. I raise myself over Caitlin, rubbing against her slit a few times.

"Ready?" I ask.

She nods, and slowly, I push inside. I watch her face as I do so, watch as her lips part and her eyes flutter closed and her hands clench the sheet.

She feels exquisite. Outside the bounds of even my overactive imagination. I move inside her, deep and slow—I can't go fast, or it'll be over too quickly. We're underneath the quilt, cocooned in our own little world, just me and Caitlin, our bodies joined. Nothing else matters.

"Good?" I murmur, and I can't help a low chuckle when she nods eagerly.

I bend down so I can kiss her lips once more. I shift down her neck, and she arches for me, letting me suck on her sensitive skin before I take her nipple in my mouth again.

It's overwhelming to have her after so long, but the most important thing is to make it good for her, to make it the best she's ever had, so that if I can give her nothing else, at least I've given her that.

As I rock my hips against her, I lower my chest to hers and feel the expanse of her skin against mine. I slip my hand between her legs to touch her clit, and her back arches, and...

"Wes!" She cries my name and holds me tight as she comes around me, and I'm a goner.

I growl and finish inside her, everything inside me expanding and then exploding.

I quickly go to the washroom to clean myself up before returning to her. Again, I'm the big spoon, but this time, we're both naked.

She giggles. "That was so much fun. I can't believe we did that."

I can hardly believe it, too.

"I've never slept with a friend before," she says.

"Neither have I."

She regards me for a moment. "Why do you never have a girlfriend?"

"I've had girlfriends."

"They don't last long, though."

It's on the tip of my tongue to confess everything. How I fell in love with her, and how that only grew as I got to know her better. The way I think everything she does is amazing.

But it's a stupid cliché to say "I love you" right after sex, isn't it?

Unlike before, I have some hope, but I want to exist in this dream world for a bit longer. Before things really change, for better or worse.

"Let's not talk about that now," I say, holding her tightly in my arms. She wiggles her ass against me again, and I know it won't be long before I'm ready to go again.

Five minutes later, however, her breathing slows and she's asleep. I inhale the scent of her hair—something floral and sophisticated—and hold her close as I join her in slumber.

•♥•♥•♥•♥•♥•

When I wake up, it's four thirty in the morning, and the light is still on.

"Morning," Caitlin says.

"Morning?" I say. "It's basically the middle of the night."

She giggles. She's been in such a giggly mood this weekend. Just for me.

I kiss her again, hoping she likes morning/middle-of-the night sex. As soon as she kisses me back, it ignites a fire within both of us, and our hands are all over each other. It's not long before I roll on a condom and push inside her from behind. At first, it's rapid, her on all fours and me pounding inside her over and over, but after she orgasms, her legs slip so she's lying on her stomach, and it's deep and languid and luxurious.

Afterward, I hold her once more, and she says something unexpected.

"I'm lonely," she admits. "Work...it's all I have. When I come home from the office, I have no one to talk to. When I have a free night, I spend it watching movies alone."

"You always have me," I say, which is as much as I can admit right now.

"I've enjoyed this weekend. I needed it. Thank you."

As I smile against the back of her neck, I realize that, in my twelve years of wanting her, I've made an error. I've thought of her as a perfect, untouchable goddess, but she's human, too. Her singing voice is absolute shit, and she snores when she sleeps, and she puts too many sprinkles on her shortbread cookies, and she's lonely. This weekend, in addition to making my fantasies come true, has also been very *real,* inflatable T-Rex costume and all.

I can make her laugh and bring her to the peak of pleasure. I would do anything for her.

Maybe I'm exactly what she needs. Those other men she dated, the ones who are nothing like me? Maybe they were all wrong for her.

She kisses my forehead. "Can I ask you a question?"

"Of course."

"What's with all the Christmas stuff? The cookies and gingerbread house and orange pomander balls…"

Not the question I was expecting.

I don't know what I was expecting, to be honest.

"Do you always do that?" she asks.

I exhale. "My mom had a health scare."

"Oh my God. I had no idea. Is she—"

"She's fine, but there were months of uncertainty." I run a hand through my hair. "She always did everything for Christmas, but this year, we're not letting her lift a finger, and it's going to be amazing."

I hug Caitlin, trying to say everything I feel with my body. Once again, she falls asleep in my arms—I can hardly believe this is becoming a regular occurrence—and I run my fingers through her hair, careful not to wake her. It's five in the morning, but I want to stay awake, to savor the feel of having her here with me.

You have to appreciate what you have. That's what the past few months have taught me. And I appreciate the hell out of having Caitlin Ng in my bed.

You also have to go for the things you want in life. Being with her, really being with her, isn't outside the realm of possibility.

When it's morning for real, I'm going to tell her the truth.

Chapter 7

Caitlin

WHEN I WAKE UP on Christmas Eve, I'm sore. I suppose this is what happens when you have sex twice in one night after not having any at all for more than a year.

It's a good kind of sore, though. I like that I can still feel Wes between my legs.

I bolt upright in bed. I slept with Wes, after deciding it was the smart and sensible solution to my problems. Oh my God, is stuff going to get strange between us now? How did that possibility not occur to me last night?

I usually think everything through. In excessive detail.

But last night, I just wanted...so I took, and pretended it was sensible.

I don't have a lot of friends. I still have a few from university, from early in my career, but now that I'm the CEO of a big dating app company, some people act weird around me.

Yeah, ironic that I'm lonely when I run a dating app. We have a friendship app now, too, because some people find that as they grow older, they lose friends (when their friends move across the country or turn out to be bigots, for example) and don't have anywhere to make new ones. It's not as big as the dating app, but it's still doing well.

I'm not on it, though, just like I'm not on Match Me.

Anyway, I don't have a lot of friends separate from work. Wes is one of them, and now we've slept together.

It didn't mean anything. I don't think sex ever means anything to Wes, and it's not like I was looking for more.

Although it was really freaking amazing.

I always thought sex would be best with someone I cared about, but last night proved that theory wrong. It was better than any sex I've had with a boyfriend.

Except I do care about Wes. Just not in that way.

Although maybe...

I shake my head. Wes is my friend, end of story, and now it might be awkward between us. Hopefully he'll know how to bridge that awkwardness—he's good at things like that.

I look over at him, asleep next to me in bed. Damn, he's gorgeous. His apartment is a proper temperature now, and he's got the sheet pushed part way down his bare chest. I remember how I ran my hands all over him last night, and I can't help a blush from creeping over my face.

How did I not realize how hot he is until last night?

As though feeling my gaze on him, he sleepily opens his eyes. "Hey, Caitlin." He smiles, doesn't bolt upright like I did. He doesn't seem bothered by waking up in bed with me.

"Hey, yourself."

"You look like you're freaking out."

"Who, me?" I laugh, but then I tell him the truth. "I don't have many friends. I can't afford to lose the ones I have. And you and I—"

"Shh." He pushes me onto my back and rolls over me. His cock is heavy between us, and his bare skin feels so good against mine.

How did I go without sex for over a year?

How did I have such good sex with a friend?

"You and I are going to be fine," he says.

And I surrender. I believe him because I need to.

I let someone else take care of things for a change.

Claudette texts me: *The power's back!* Since it stopped snowing a while ago and the streets downtown have mostly been cleared, I could go home.

But I don't.

Because I like spending time with Wes.

There are more Christmas preparations today. I remember what he told me in the middle of the night about his mom. I'm so glad she's okay, and I feel like a shitty friend—I didn't know any of this was going on. I need to make more of an effort with the friends I do have, though Wes hasn't reached out to me as much as usual in the past few months, either.

Now, he swipes up some chocolate ganache—a mixture of chocolate and cream—on his finger and slips it between my lips. When I swirl my tongue around his finger, he moans.

It's been different between us all morning. He's been touching me casually, randomly planting kisses on my cheeks and neck, feeding me bits of the food we're making. Right now, we're making chocolate truffles.

We haven't gone back to the way we were before. We've slipped into couple behavior instead, and I have to say, I like it. I've missed moments like these.

Moments when I'm hanging out with a guy in my kitchen, licking chocolate off his fingers, and he moans and says, "I can't help thinking of your mouth in other places."

Exactly what was on my mind.

Somehow this leads to me giving him a blow job and us having sex on a chair in the kitchen. Funny how making chocolate truffles can lead to such activities.

Then we have a shower together. It's only sensible, since we both need to get clean and he only has one shower, right?

Usually, getting distracted like that is unthinkable for me. I get shit done.

But today, with Wes, it's okay to live differently. It's a nice change from my usual life.

Once all of the ganache has been rolled into balls (balls—tee-hee), it goes back in the fridge to harden. (Harden, lol. My mind is in the gutter today.) In a little while, we'll take it back out and roll the truffles in cocoa powder, chopped pistachios, and shredded coconut.

For now, though, we decorate the tree. It's been up in Wes's apartment the entire time I've been here, but with only lights and a star on top—no other decorations. He has a wide variety of ornaments, including some adorable ones that were clearly made by his little niece and nephew.

My heart squeezes. I don't have any nieces or nephews, and I have no family here for Christmas.

I take a deep breath. It's okay. I'm hanging out with Wes now, and we're having a good time enjoying the holiday season—and each other's bodies.

Suddenly, I picture him doing this with another woman, though perhaps that's stupid. Wes isn't one for relationships. But maybe he makes chocolate truffles or gingerbread cookies with all of his flings. Maybe he's been sweet and romantic like this with dozens of other women, women who are much easier to be with than me.

I'm aware that I intimidate men. Many men would be fine with a woman who makes a little more than them, but I'm a CEO, and that's a different story. I'm freakishly driven, and I work too hard, though this weekend has shown me that I need to give myself more breaks. Just having a weekend off work is a revelation.

I usually date high-powered men who are attracted to my success, but once we start getting serious, they want me to be someone other than who I am. One wanted me to be more glamorous, the perfect arm candy; another expected me to quit my job once we had kids.

Wes has never acted weird around me, though. Right now, I'm not some overworked CEO; I'm just a woman enjoying the holiday season with a man.

I put a Santa ornament on the tree and turn toward Wes. He grins and steps toward me, slipping his arm around my hip.

He may claim he doesn't do relationships, but one day, he will find someone. I'm sure of it. He's such a good guy, and he's easy to talk to, and it's so easy for me to picture him being someone's boyfriend.

I push those thoughts aside and restrain myself from stabbing my hand with an icicle ornament.

"Hey," Wes whispers, in a voice that makes me all gooey inside. "I'm going to pop out to get something. I'll be back in twenty minutes, okay?"

"What are you getting?"

"You'll see." He winks.

Hmm. I wonder where he's going?

Chapter 8

Wes

Excellent. The small grocer on the corner has mistletoe.

I remember seeing it when I walked by a few days ago and I feared they might have sold it all by now, but it's still here. I buy some, make another purchase at Happy as Pie in Baldwin Village, and head back to my apartment building.

It still seems like a bit of a longshot, but I'm going to confess my feelings for Caitlin Ng, and I'm going to do it under the mistletoe. Is that a bit of a cliché? I don't know, but it's the best idea I have.

Maybe I can be what she needs, and maybe she feels the same way about me, even though she said it was just sex.

But after last night...it's hard to believe she didn't feel it, too.

I grin. I had Caitlin in my bed last night, and this morning, and we weren't just "snuggling for warmth."

I was inside her, and it was everything I'd imagined and more.

I'm still grinning like a fool when I walk into the apartment and see her there, looking like she belongs. I hang up the mistletoe in the bedroom doorway and then I take her hand and lead her under it.

Although I'm happy, I'm also freaking the fuck out, because I'm finally, after a dozen years, going to say something to Caitlin.

But first, I'm going to kiss her.

I point up at the mistletoe and waggle my eyebrows, trying to act like casual, easygoing Wes, even if that's not how I feel right now. "Looks like it's time for us to kiss."

Caitlin frowns. "That's not mistletoe."

"It's not?"

She chuckles. "It's holly. Did you go out to get mistletoe just for an excuse to kiss me, and then end up buying holly?"

I grab my phone and look up mistletoe.

She's right. Of course she's right; this is Caitlin, after all.

Why did I always think this was mistletoe? I have no idea. Though frankly, mistletoe is pretty plain. How did something so plain become a Christmas tradition?

I'm not embarrassed when I dance around a pub in a T-Rex costume to Christmas songs, but I'm embarrassed now. Embarrassed that I'm such an idiot.

A reminder I needed, perhaps.

Sure, Caitlin and I shared a bed, and sure, I can show her a good time, and sure, I can be her friend, but I'm not her type.

Her type? Men who wouldn't be so stupid as to mix up mistletoe and holly. I've met a few of her exes, and they're nothing like me. And surely Caitlin knows what kind of guy she wants.

It was stupid to ever think that was an option.

So I abort my mission. I leave the holly hanging in the doorway, and I kiss Caitlin anyway, but I don't share the feelings I've been concealing for years.

When we walk back to the table to finish up the truffles, I do another search on my phone. I find numerous people saying how stupid it is to confuse mistletoe with holly and how such idiots should be stabbed in the eye with prickly holly leaves.

Well. Great to know that people like me inspire such violent thoughts.

After we finish the truffles, I make Caitlin some tea because her hands are cold and she says she's had enough hot chocolate for the weekend, though I'm not sure how anyone can ever have too much hot chocolate. I also bring out the box I bought from Happy as Pie.

"It's the best key lime pie I've ever had," I say, opening up the box. "You have to try it."

"Key lime pie is my favorite!" she says. "You remembered."

Yes, of course I remembered. I remember everything about her.

As we're sitting at my tiny kitchen table, sipping tea and eating pie and shortbread cookies, she reaches over and squeezes my hand.

"Thank you," she says. "I didn't think a snowstorm and losing power at my house would lead to such a great weekend, but it did. I'm not looking forward to spending Christmas alone."

"What about your parents?"

"They're in Hong Kong."

I can't allow Caitlin to spend Christmas by herself. That's unthinkable. Especially since she admitted last night that she's lonely.

"You can celebrate Christmas with my family," I say. "This evening. Then you can spend the night here again, if you like."

"Really? I don't want to intrude."

"No, no. It's fine. There will be a ton of food—look at all the dessert we've made." I sweep my arm across the kitchen, where there are tins of cookies and truffles and a rather hideous gingerbread house that's lacking structural stability. "My father bought a twenty-pound turkey, which is a lot when there's only five adults, a four-year-old, and a toddler who only eats mac and cheese."

"If you're sure," she says doubtfully.

"Yes, I'm absolutely sure. You can come to our Christmas Eve dinner."

My mother will ask hopeful questions, since I'm bringing a girl—she hasn't met Caitlin, or most of my friends from university before—but it's nothing I can't handle.

Caitlin stands up abruptly, knocking the table in the process. "I should go to the mall to get presents. What does your niece like? Your nephew? What should I get your parents?"

"You don't need to go to the mall on one of the worst shopping days of the year. I have lots of presents. They won't expect you to bring anything."

She sits back down. "I can't show up empty-handed."

"You won't. You'll be helping me carry everything." I sweep my hand across the room again. "You can carry the gingerbread house."

She gives me a look. "You know what I mean."

"You don't have to be perfect."

"I'm not trying to be perfect. I'm trying to be courteous."

"I'll add your name to all the labels on the presents, what about that?"

"Then it'll be like we're a couple, but we're not." She picks up a gingerbread cookie and bites off the head. "Sometimes I give interviews, talking about how I believe in love and how we can help people find it, sharing success stories—I love reading those. But..." She shakes her head. "People talk about me as though I'm amazing, a young minority woman who started this company from nothing and is now a CEO, but sometimes I feel like a fraud."

"Because you run a dating website, but you don't have anyone for yourself?"

Me! Me! a part of my brain screams. *Pick me!*

I push that aside. I decided I wouldn't say anything, and so I won't. Caitlin isn't some perfect being who's on a plane above everyone else. She's a woman who snores and can't sing—as I discovered this weekend.

Still, I'm not her type.

"Well, that, too..." she begins, "but mostly, I just feel like it was all a fluke."

I give her a look. "It was not all a fluke. You did it because you're smart, and you were able to figure out what people wanted and needed."

"As a twenty-five-year-old single woman in the city when I was starting out, it was easy to figure out what women could use."

"But nobody else did what you did." I put my hands on her shoulders. "Just because there was some luck involved doesn't mean it was all a fluke. You're brilliant, and you would have done something like that eventually, I know it."

She smiles weakly at me.

I need her to understand. "I believe in you. I always did. From the moment you knocked me in the head with a door, I knew you were going to do great things in life." I pause. "Imagine you're some white dude from a big-name family who went to prep school then an Ivy League college. You'd be so fucking full of yourself, you would *never* think it was a fluke, or that it had anything to do with all the advantages you received in life. You would wake up in the morning, cocky as shit, and think, "I'm awesome!""

She laughs, just a little, and then she bends over and laughs really fucking hard, and she's so pretty when she laughs like that—it hits me in the chest.

"Thanks," she says. "I'm sorry. I know it's ridiculous for me to be insecure and suffer from imposter syndrome when—"

I put a finger to her lips. "Don't apologize for anything, not with me. One day, you'll have the fairy tale that you help other people find. I know it. Because in addition to everything else, you're really amazing in bed. I have first-hand experience."

She laughs again, and I look away, swallowing hard.

I have no doubt that she'll find someone eventually, but it won't be me.

Chapter 9

Caitlin

"Why are you bringing your T-Rex costume?" I ask as we carry the second round of boxes and bags down to Wes's car.

"To surprise Dana, my niece," he says. "She loves dinosaurs."

"I assume one of these poorly wrapped boxes contains a dinosaur-related present for her." I've been teasing him about his wrapping skills all day.

"Of course. Books and dinosaur toys—she was particularly keen on getting a pachycephalosaurus this year. She borrowed my sister's phone three times to call me and ask me to buy her one."

If my ovaries were the twitching sort, they would probably be twitching now.

We load everything into Wes's clunker of a car, including the box of persimmons that I insisted on buying for his parents, and drive to Scarborough. I can't help feeling nervous, as though I'm meeting a boyfriend's family for the first time.

We turn into the driveway of his parents' suburban house, and as soon as Wes hops out of the car, he strips off his winter jacket and toque and scarf, even though we're not inside yet.

"I'm putting on the T-Rex costume now," he says.

I help him into the costume, then put a poinsettia garland around T-Rex's neck and a Santa hat, which has long strings to tie under the chin, on the dinosaur's head. He picks up a small bag of presents, I pick up the box of persimmons, and we go to the door and knock.

A woman who must be Wes's sister, Lia, opens the door, a little girl and boy beside her.

"Ho, ho, ho," Wes says. "Merry Christmas!"

Dana shrieks. "Mommy, it's a Christmas dinosaur!"

The little boy—Owen, who's nearly three—starts crying, and Dana rolls her eyes and scolds her brother. "It's not a real dinosaur, dummy. It's not big enough!"

Owen is inconsolable. "The dinosaur ate Santa!"

Wes points to his face through the clear window on the dinosaur's neck.

Dana shrieks again with glee. "Uncle Wes!"

"Dinosaur ate Uncle Wes!" Owen is still crying.

The next five minutes are rather surreal. Wes growls and chases Dana around the house, and Owen is repeatedly assured that it's only a fake, vegetarian T-Rex. Wes's parents emerge and shake their heads.

After Wes takes off the costume, everyone finally notices that he's brought a guest.

"This is Caitlin," he says. "Caitlin, these are my parents, Thomas and Audrey."

"You didn't tell me you were bringing a girl," Audrey says. "How wonderful! So many years of you showing up alone. I had given up hope."

"Caitlin isn't my girlfriend. She's my friend, and she has nobody to spend Christmas with this year."

Audrey's expression turns to one of crushing disappointment. "If only you had stayed an engineer, then you would find a nice woman! I told you not to quit that job. Most women would be happy with an engineer. Better than a freelance graphic designer." She clucks her tongue.

"Mom, please," Lia says. "Not this again, okay?" She turns to me. "What do you do?"

"I studied computer engineering with Wes," I say, deciding to be vague.

Wes doesn't say anything, letting me introduce myself however I like, but Lia taps her finger against her lips. "You look familiar. Really familiar. Wait, I know!" She whips out her phone and pulls up an article. "You're Caitlin Ng! I've read about you."

"You're famous?" Audrey peers at my face.

"She started a really big dating app. Called Match Me. Some of my friends use it."

Thomas also takes out his phone and looks me up. "She's rich!"

"How much is she worth?" Audrey demands.

"Okay, okay," Wes says. "Everybody calm down. Yes, Caitlin is a CEO, but she's also my friend, alright?"

Audrey clucks her tongue again. "You started a dating app, but you have no man to spend Christmas with, only your friend? That seems like bad advertising."

"Mom, please interrogate me instead of Caitlin, okay?"

"I know what it is! You're not friends with Wes. You hired him. Like an escort! I read a book about this, about a rich woman who hired an escort to give her love lessons. It was very hot, actually"—she fans herself with her hand—"but that's not what I want for my son! He has an engineering degree! No need to sell his body."

I'm getting whiplash from this conversation.

"How do you sell your body?" Dana asks with wide-eyed curiosity. "How does that work?"

"Why don't you go off and play with your brother?" Lia suggests, shooing her away.

"Look," I say, composing myself. "It's exactly as Wes says. We're friends from university. Nothing more complicated than that." I remember Wes licking between my legs last night, and I feel a rush of heat, but I press on. "I don't understand why you want him to work as an engineer. He was miserable. Why do you want him to be miserable?"

"Don't approve of these New Age ideas," Thomas says. "Life isn't all about being happy."

I'm not surprised by any of this—my parents aren't all that different—but still. Wes has nothing to be ashamed of. Sure, he's not a doctor like his sister, and his apartment and car aren't anything fancy, but he has a career and he does okay for himself. He seems happy with the choice he's made, which is a far cry from the Wes I met in university. I'm glad he figured everything out.

Audrey lets out an unexpected laugh. "You *are* dating. You're definitely dating. That's why you stick up for him like that. Good, good."

Wes and I share a look.

Which, perhaps, isn't making us seem like less of a couple.

"Mom," he says. "Like I said, we're not together."

I feel a pang in my heart.

Maybe I do want to be a couple after all.

Wes carves the turkey, and I can't help admiring his arm muscles when he pushes up his sleeves.

"Caitlin," he murmurs. "You checking me out?"

His mother couldn't have heard that, but she looks up sharply from the other side of the kitchen, and when she makes a comment a few minutes later about us being together, I don't protest. I don't want to. Wes doesn't protest, either, and that thrills me, though maybe he's just keeping quiet because he's tired of correcting his mom.

Dinner is delicious. I've only had turkey with stuffing a couple of times before. In my family, we go to a Chinese restaurant for Christmas dinner, which is what we do for basically every holiday, including Thanksgiving. We don't buy a turkey, and besides, a turkey would be too much for the three of us.

"When we were little, we used to do that, too," Lia says, after asking me what my family does for Christmas. "Then Dad decided that since we were in Canada now, we should have a turkey."

"Of course, I was the one who had to make it," Audrey says. "I underestimated how much time it would take to cook. It went back into the oven so many times, and we didn't eat until ten o'clock at night."

"But it was really good." Wes smiles. "So now we do it every year."

"Well, *I* was the one who did it every year until today." Audrey looks at Thomas. "Apparently the key to getting everyone else to do the work is to get sick and make people think you're dying, then fool them all by being healthy! They get scared of losing you, and they don't take you for granted anymore."

"Mom." Wes reaches across the table and pats her hand.

"My son made a whole gingerbread house! He's not a good engineer, but he can make a tasty gingerbread house. I snuck a piece before dinner."

"In all honesty," Lia says, "it's a little ugly."

"Function is better than form." Audrey nods decisively. "Turkey stuffing? It looks like dog food, but it's delicious." She holds up a forkful. "And it was so nice of you to bring a pretty girl with you, Wes. That is the best part. Maybe you will get married after all!"

I choke on my turkey and cranberry sauce, and Wes puts his hand on my leg. I want him, yes, but I'm not ready to think about marriage yet.

Once dinner is finished and half of the gingerbread house has been demolished and Devon, Lia's husband, arrives after his shift at the hospital, the presents are opened. Dana loves pachycephalosaurus. Wes got her two, and she keeps slamming their heads together, saying it's a widely known fact that pachycephalosauruses butted heads.

Dana also gets a book about dinosaurs that looks rather scientific for a four-year-old, but she's thrilled and immediately asks Wes to read it to her, then critiques his pronunciation of "coelophysis" and "compsognathus."

"How does she know how to pronounce these words?" he asks his sister.

"She doesn't. She just knows you're pronouncing them differently than I do."

"If she likes long scientific words," Audrey says, "you should teach her anatomy. It will be useful when she goes to med school."

"Mom!" Lia says. "She's four."

"I'm kidding!"

"I want to be a paleontologist," Dana announces.

"My neighbor Claudette was a paleontologist," I tell her, and Dana thinks this is the coolest thing ever.

"Mommy." Owen frowns. "Why did I get pillows?"

"Um, sweetie," Lia says, "that present wasn't for you. You shouldn't have opened it. Bring it over here for Uncle Wes. They're throw pillows for his ugly futon, to make it look sophisticated."

I don't have any presents to open, but I don't mind. I like being with Wes's family. They aren't perfect—whose family is?—but I find myself wanting to do this again. Wanting to come here for Chinese New Year and Easter and whenever his family gets together.

And most of all, wanting to be with Wes. When I see him reading the dinosaur book to his rapt audience, I get a strange stirring in my chest.

The feeling of wanting to be a real couple? It has only intensified over the evening.

Lia's family is staying overnight so the kids can have Christmas morning and presents from Santa with their grandparents. Devon suggests that Santa is probably sick of getting cookies and milk at every house, and why don't they put out a whole-wheat muffin for Santa instead? Owen starts crying at the thought of poor Santa having to eat a healthy muffin, and eventually they agree that Santa can have a couple of White Rabbit candies and shortbread cookies. Even though we all ate a ton, there's still a lot left.

Wes and I head home around nine—and by "home," I mean we go to his apartment.

"I don't want you to spend Christmas morning alone," he murmurs.

No, I certainly don't want that, either.

As soon as we enter his apartment, he hoists me into his arms—no small feat, given all the turkey and stuffing and gingerbread I consumed—and carries me to the bedroom. He undresses me and lays me on top of the comforter.

Today, unlike the other night, it's warm enough in here for me to be naked without any covers. His gaze travels over me as he pulls off his sweater and T-shirt, followed by his jeans.

I nearly start drooling when he crawls toward me on the bed, wearing only his boxers. I might be stuffed, but he looks good enough to eat.

"Caitlin," he says, "this is the best Christmas present a guy could ask for."

He holds himself above me. So close, but not a single inch of his skin is touching me, and I whimper. I want him. I want to feel him inside me. Tonight, and tomorrow.

Again, and again, and again.

I want to come home from a long day at work and find him waiting for me, maybe in this outfit, pulling a batch of cookies out of the oven.

I want to wake up next to him and start the day by making love to him.

Making love.

When we first had sex, I wasn't thinking about that at all, but even though I kept telling myself it didn't mean anything, it did. Sleeping with my friend, a dozen years after we met for the first time, was not just about scratching an itch, and sex changed things even more.

Wes has always been there for me, always understood me, and I'm so grateful to have him in my life. The guys

I've dated before were, in some ways, more similar to me, but they were wrong. All wrong. I see that now.

Still holding himself above me, Wes runs the tip of his finger over my entrance, to my clit, and I whimper again.

He grins wickedly and lifts his hand from my body.

"Wes!" I squirm.

"You're so pretty like that," he says. "When you're desperate to be filled with my cock."

The first time I was naked in front of him, I was shy. Vulnerable.

But not now.

Well, I *am* vulnerable, but in a different way from before.

He sheds his boxers and crawls up my body until his erection bobs in front of my mouth. When I put my lips on him and suck, he groans.

He's desperate for me, too.

No other man will do for me, and I wonder if no other woman will do for him. Perhaps it's conceited of me to think that, but I can't help it.

He lies down on his back and puts on a condom. "Come sit."

I ease myself down onto his cock and groan as he fills me, one inch at a time. No, it has never been like this with anyone else, not for me. We move in perfect harmony as we kiss, and it feels so right.

All I want for Christmas is for this to never end.

That's a pretty big Christmas gift, though.

He keeps thrusting inside me as he rolls us over so he's on top. His strokes are deep and overwhelming and utterly perfect.

Yes, there is absolutely nothing I want more than him.

He kisses my mouth, my temple, my neck, my breasts. He lavishes attention on every part of me, and when he touches my clit, I shudder and cry out his name, and then he comes inside me.

We hold each other afterward, as we always do. Is this how he is with other women? I can't bear to think of him being with anyone else.

I want him all to myself.

Tomorrow. Tomorrow I will tell him how I feel, and God, I hope he feels the same way. I'm not in the habit of waiting for someone else to say something—I go after what I want.

And more than anything, I want Wes.

I want to spend Christmas with him every year.

Chapter 10

Wes

For the third day in a row, I wake up with Caitlin in my bed.

For the second day in a row, I wake up with a *naked* Caitlin in my bed.

I don't understand how a guy like me could get so fucking lucky, but somehow, it's happened. She's here. It's the stuff of my dreams.

"Merry Christmas, Caitlin," I say when her eyes flutter open. I brush my lips over her cheek, and she smiles at me, all dopey-eyed and beautiful.

I kiss my way down her neck, and I'm about to reach between her legs when she stills my hand. "I want to ask you something first."

I bring my hands back to her shoulders. "What's up?"

She worries her bottom lip between her teeth. It's not like her to be nervous like this.

"I want you," she says. "I want a relationship with you."

I go utterly still. "You want a relationship. With me?" I repeat stupidly, my voice going high-pitched.

"I do."

Yes, we've been great in bed together. Yes, the past few days have been amazing, and that single question is everything I've wanted since the first week of university all those years ago.

I'd planned to ask her yesterday, and now she's asked me instead.

Caitlin Ng wants me, or at least she thinks she does. For now.

"I'm not your type," I point out. "I'm nothing like the other guys you've dated."

"Maybe my type has changed."

Caitlin's a success story, and I'm not. My sister is a doctor who married a doctor and has two adorable kids—I'm the screw-up in the family. Always have been, as last night reminded me. Caitlin was lovely and stuck up for me and said I shouldn't do anything that made me miserable, but...

No, I can't let her do this.

"You're too good for me," I say, because in the end, that's what it comes down to. I may talk about "types" and all that, but I've known from the beginning that she deserves better than me, and there's no way she'll stay interested in the long-term.

"Wes." She laughs uncomfortably. "That's ridiculous. You're a good man, a caring man. You didn't make a great computer engineer, but you're smart and creative and hot as fuck."

I can't help laughing at that, even though I feel hollow on the inside.

Caitlin and I have laughed a lot together this weekend.

"I was the perfect fling for you," I say, "but we're better off as friends."

"Stop being an idiot."

I can't. It's just who I am.

I take a few deep breaths. God, I want to pull her back into my arms and tell her yes, I want her, I can be what she needs. I love her more than anything; I've always loved her.

But I say nothing.

"Oh," she says quietly. "I see. Close your eyes."

"Why?"

"So you can't watch when I climb out of bed naked to get dressed."

We've spent so much time without our clothes on in the past few days, but all good things must come to an end.

I do as she requests.

· ❤ · ❤ · ❤ · ❤ · ❤ ·

Twenty minutes later, I'm sipping a cup of coffee and looking morosely at my festive Christmas tree, which *she* helped me decorate. The last few days have shown me that being with Caitlin is indeed as amazing as I always imagined it would be.

And so, because she is wonderful and amazing and fantastic and sexy, I must let her go, so she can find some CEO to make little CEO babies with. Some cocky white dude who thinks he's all that and doesn't dance around in an inflatable T-Rex costume on Christmas Day.

Because that's how I'm going to spend the afternoon.

I look at the holly—not mistletoe—hanging in my bedroom door, and the container of shortbread and gingerbread cookies on the counter. All things that remind me of her.

I haven't eaten breakfast. I'm not hungry. I assume that has something to do with heartbreak and consuming a week's worth of food last night.

Still, I'm craving sugar right now, and I might as well console myself by stuffing cookies into my face. I'm just being festive, right?

Merry fucking Christmas to me.

I drain my cup of coffee, then make myself a mocha—gotta get my sugar in liquid form, too—with a generous amount of Bailey's. I take a bite of a shortbread

Santa, which has an excessive amount of sprinkles, thanks to Caitlin, and try not to start weeping.

I've had years of practice at burying my feelings for her. I should be able to do this. Though no matter how deep I try to bury them, they always manage to pop up again.

And now I know what it's like to snuggle her for warmth...and to snuggle her just because. Now I know what it feels like to be inside her. Now I know what it feels like to make a gingerbread house with her, to pepper her with kisses throughout the day.

Oh, God, I'm so screwed.

But it's Christmas Day, and I have a job to do. I've got to wear a T-Rex costume and dance to Christmas songs sung by a barbershop quartet.

I'm such a weirdo, I know.

A noble weirdo: I let Caitlin go.

It's for the best, isn't it? She'll see that soon enough.

Chapter 11

Caitlin

I RARELY LET MYSELF burst into tears, even when everything seems impossible.

But when I collapse on my expensive sectional couch in my living room, I let the tears come.

I have nearly everything I could want in life, including more money than I need. No, I can't afford a private jet and have it take me around the world, but who the hell needs a private jet? I own a nice house in Cabbagetown—I've always loved the old Victorian houses here. It's not as big as what I could have bought. I'm only one person; why do I need a mansion?

I have a nice house, and I take nice vacations, though I usually spend half of them on my laptop and phone.

But money can't buy the love of the man I want.

I start crying harder as I realize the truth: I love Wes.

Most people think I'm smart, but I must be pretty stupid not to have seen what was right in front of my face.

Wes is amazing and I've known him for years—how did it take me so long?

He doesn't feel the same way about me, though.

Oh, sure, he claimed I was too good for him, but he was just trying to let me down gently. I didn't realize it at first; I told him to stop being an idiot.

But then everything slipped into place. He likes me as a friend, and he's happy for me to warm his bed, but he's not interested in anything more.

That happens. I run a dating site; I know feelings and attraction can be one-sided.

I've gotten far in life by working hard, but hard work won't get me Wes Cheng.

I need to move on.

Unfortunately, I doubt I'll be interested in picking someone up at Eugene's party next week. I won't be ready to take my clothes off for a new guy by then. I'll ring in the New Year without anyone to kiss, and I'll spend the rest of Christmas alone.

I head upstairs to take a shower, and as the warm water sluices over my skin, I take deep breaths and tell myself it'll all be okay.

I'm Caitlin Ng, and I can conquer the world.

After I get dressed, I call Eugene—who doesn't celebrate Christmas, so he's not busy today—to tell him I'm going to his party on New Year's Eve.

"I know," he says. "You texted me on Thursday."

"Did I?" Man, I'm so out of it.

"Yeah, you sure did. What's up?"

For some reason, it all just comes pouring out of me. The snowstorm, going to Wes's apartment. Eugene laughs his head off at the "snuggling for warmth" part. It's good to talk to someone who's known both of us for twelve long years.

Then I get to this morning. I tell Eugene about how I took a risk and told Wes what I wanted.

"But he shot me down." I sigh. "He was trying to be nice, saying I was too good for him, but I know he just doesn't feel that way about me. Even though, dammit—"

"No, he's in love with you," Eugene says. "He's always been in love with you."

"That makes no sense."

"I can't believe you never noticed. He thinks he's good at hiding it, but he's not. Why do you think he's never had a relationship that lasted more than a month? Because none of those women were you, and you're the only one he wants."

My head is spinning. Wes has *always* been in love with me?

No, that couldn't be.

"This is all conjecture on your part," I say.

"No, it's not. After many years of watching this farce, I confronted him last year, and he told me the same thing he told you—that you were too good for him, and he could never say anything. He said you needed some guy who could buy you diamond necklaces and whisk you away to Paris for a weekend."

"I don't want any of that," I protest. "I mean, I can afford those things myself. I don't need a man for that. I need a guy to make me laugh and remind me not to work for twelve hours straight and get me to help him make a gingerbread house that teeters on the brink of collapse. I need a guy I can really talk to and be with just as a regular woman, not a CEO."

I'm the woman who understands exactly what other women wanted in their love lives, yet could never sort out her own. I was never quite sure of what I wanted in a man.

Until now.

"Wes has never been weird around me because of my success," I say. "That's one of the things I like about him, but you're saying he truly thinks I'm too good for him?"

"I'm pretty sure he always thought that. Not just in the past five years...when we were students, too. All the hotshots you dated in the past few years probably didn't help, though to be honest, as successful as they were, most of them were pretty annoying."

I want to pull out my hair. Wes is such an infuriating man.

Still, I love him, and I'm giddy with the thought that he might love me, too.

I rein in my feelings and try to think logically.

Okay. All is not lost. I just need to get him to stop being a bonehead. I've done many difficult things in life. This should be manageable.

"Thank you," I tell Eugene, then end the phone call.

Hopefully, when I go to Eugene's party next weekend, it will be with Wes by my side. But first, I need a really good plan...

I snap my fingers. Got it. The only problem is that it's Christmas and nearly everything is closed. Where can I get a T-Rex costume at this late hour?

Ah. I know who might own one.

Chapter 12

Wes

We're about halfway through our engagements for the afternoon. Me and the barbershop quartet, that is. We've already performed at two nursing homes, and the children's rehabilitation hospital is next. Bernie's son, who's older than my father, is driving us around in his van. Bernie is up front, Paul (the lead) and Billy (the tenor) are in the next row, and Henry (the baritone) is sitting next to me in the back.

"We need to talk," Henry says to me. At ninety, he's the oldest in the group.

"You breaking up with me?" I say jokingly.

Henry's face turns serious.

Shit. Maybe they really have decided that they don't need a dancing T-Rex anymore.

"Henry," Paul hisses. "You promised you wouldn't say anything."

Henry ignores him. "Your performance isn't up to your usual standards," he tells me. "Yes, it's a T-Rex costume, so it's still hilarious, but you looked like a depressed T-Rex during 'Angels We Have Heard on High.' It didn't fit the spirit of the song."

He has a point. I've been going through the motions today. I'm not in the mood for Christmas after turning down Caitlin this morning. I didn't think anyone would notice, though, since I'm wearing a gigantic costume much of the time.

But everyone murmurs their agreement.

"We'd appreciate if you could take things up a notch," Bernie says, "but more than anything, we're concerned about you. Why are you in a bad mood on Christmas?"

Four elderly men stare at me through their glasses.

"Um." I scratch the back of my neck. "It's nothing."

"No, it's something," Henry says.

"Lady troubles." Billy nods sagely. "I bet that's it."

"That woman who came to our performance during the snowstorm," Bernie says. "It's her, isn't it? She turn you down?"

"No," I say miserably. "She wants to be with me."

"And what's the problem?" Henry asks. "You don't like her that way, and you had to let her down easy?"

"You were afraid you wouldn't be able to...perform?" Billy asks. "You know there's Viagra for that."

"Billy!" Paul says. "He's thirty years old, not ninety. I don't think that's a concern."

This is followed by a five-minute conversation about erections and aging, which I can't say I needed, but I'm not cringing near as much as Bernie's son, who finally cuts Bernie off by shouting, "I don't need to learn about my father's sex life!"

"Okay, okay," Bernie says. "Between the five of us, we have over four hundred years of life experience. Surely we can help you sort this out. What's the problem with this nice young lady wanting to be with you?"

"She's too good for me. I'm nothing like the guys she's dated."

"Is she a princess?" Billy asks, with complete seriousness.

"No, she's a CEO."

"Women can do anything these days," Paul says. "I mean, they always could, we just tried to stop them. My granddaughter Libby is a surgeon!"

They spend the next five minutes bragging about their granddaughters, which is much better than listening to them talk about erections.

Finally, Bernie says, "Enough! Back to Wes's problem." He turns to me. "You need to get your head out of your ass, young man. Who are you to decide that you're too good for her? She already decided that's not true. Listen to her." The other men murmur their agreement. "I know how you feel, though. I thought my Margaret was too good for me, too. But did I sulk around in an inflatable dinosaur costume? No. I asked her to marry me, and I've spent every day since—three hundred and sixty five days times sixty-five years—showing that I love her and proving that I deserve her. I might be a crotchety old man, but I believe she made the right choice, because nobody loves her like I do."

"That was really touching, Dad," his son says.

They continue to talk, but I'm not really listening.

Bernie's right. Who am I to tell Caitlin that she doesn't know what's best for her, when she knows herself better than anyone? The woman I love is incredibly smart, and if she thinks we would make a good couple, then I'm sure she's right. And she deserves better than to be subjected to my insecurities.

Instead of slinking away, I'm going to be the man she deserves. I'm going to be proud of what I've made of myself.

"Could you let me off right here?" I ask. "I have a woman to win back."

"No way," Bernie says. "You're coming to our last performance. We're counting on you. Seriously, Wes, it's a children's rehab hospital. Don't bail on the children!"

Well, okay. He's right. I must fulfill my obligations, and then I'm going to see Caitlin.

"But good for you for getting your head out of your ass."

·♥·♥·♥·♥·♥·

I dance my heart out for the children and their parents. After we finish our set—to lots of applause—I get Bernie's son to drop me off in Chinatown, and all the old men insist on waiting for me. Not much is open on Christmas, but you can depend on a few places in Chinatown to be open. I buy a little present for Caitlin, plus a red box to put it in.

I think of her strutting around my kitchen, singing "All I Want for Christmas Is You" a little off-tune, and the way she dumped too many sprinkles on the shortbread cookies.

I think of how cool and professional she looks when she does interviews on TV.

I was going to tell her the truth yesterday, but then I freaked out when I mixed up mistletoe and holly. It's no big deal that I didn't know the difference, yet I foolishly used it as proof that I wasn't good enough for her.

Now, for the first time in a dozen years, I truly believe we have a chance. I believe I can be the right man for her.

What if I'd said something to Caitlin when we were in undergrad?

I don't know. She might not have been able to think of me this way back then. Or maybe we'd be celebrating our tenth Christmas together.

But enough about the might-have-beens. I'm going to make this right.

I hope she'll have me, after I broke her heart on Christmas morning, of all times. I think she will, but I can't be absolutely sure.

One thing I do know: I'll always love her. I tried keeping my distance, and that didn't change my feelings. Nothing will.

I get back in the van and direct Bernie's son to Caitlin's house in Cabbagetown, while the men all argue about what I should tell Caitlin and whether or not I should put on the T-Rex costume.

"You should get down on one knee!" Henry says.

"No, he should not," Billy says. "She'll think he's proposing, and it might scare her."

At long last, we reach Caitlin's. I climb out of the van and think, what the hell, I'll put on the costume, even though it's a bit of a hassle. But it's what I was wearing on Saturday, when we saw each other for the first time in months, and it's something none of her exes would have done.

The idea that I might be able to wake up next to her every day seems almost too good to be true, but I get into the T-Rex costume, wave at the barbershop quartet, and make my way to Caitlin's porch, heart beating far too fast.

I can do this. I can do this.

If only she'll have me back, I'll make her the very best triple-story gingerbread house next year, I'll cook her a five-course dinner for her birthday, I'll give her as many orgasms as I can, and I'll snuggle her for warmth every night this winter.

I'm about to ring the doorbell when the door swings open and I find myself face-to-face with a T-Rex—the exact same inflatable costume as my own. In shock, I'm unable to move my feet, and the T-Rex knocks into me.

"What the..." The voice is muffled, but it's unmistakably Caitlin.

This isn't going how I expected, but that's okay. I take a deep breath and find my voice. "I'm so sorry about this morning. The truth is that I've been in love with you for twelve years, and for all of those twelve years, I believed I wasn't your type and you were out of my league, so I didn't say anything."

"I know," she says, surprising me. "Eugene told me."

Wait a second.

If Caitlin is wearing a T-Rex costume, that can only mean one thing. I doubt she'd put one on just for shits on Christmas Day. She was...

"I was coming to find you," she says, "and tell you that I'm most definitely not too good for you. When you turned me down, I didn't believe you meant that. I thought you were trying to let me down easy and spare my feelings."

"No, not at all. I really believed that, but I've come to see I was wrong. I was being stupidly insecure." I let out a breath. "But you deserve better than a stupidly insecure guy—and I can be the man-slash-T-Rex you need. As the past few days have shown, we're great together. Just as great as I'd always imagined we'd be, but I'd never dared to hope it was possible."

We embrace, the heads of our costumes bumping awkwardly together, and somewhere in the background, a barbershop quartet starts singing "I've Got My Love to Keep Me Warm."

I turn around and see Bernie, Paul, Billy, and Henry standing in front of the van.

"Be careful you don't slip!" shouts Bernie's son. "The last thing we need on Christmas is for someone to bust their hip."

"Okay, guys," I say. "Thank you for the words of wisdom earlier, but I've got it covered now."

They switch to singing "I'll Be Home for Christmas" as they struggle to climb back into the van. A couple minutes later, they're safely off, and Caitlin and I are alone. I can just imagine the sight we make, both dressed up as T-Rexes.

"Nice costume," I say. "Where did you get it?"

She gestures to the house next to hers. There's a head poking up from behind a curtain, but it quickly disappears. "My paleontologist neighbor. Now take your head out of the dinosaur's neck so you can kiss me."

Soon, my lips are on hers, those lips that looked so kissable the first time I saw them all those years ago. They are, indeed, as wonderful as I imagined they'd be. I pull her as close as I can with the bulk of the costumes.

It's Christmas, and we're together, and it's amazing.

Inside her house, we take off our costumes and I give Caitlin her present. She opens the box, revealing a pair of New Year's headbands.

"I want to be the man you kiss at midnight," I say. "The man you take home with you. This year, and the year after, and the year after that..."

"I can't believe you've been in love with me all this time." She shakes her head. "All these years and you never said anything."

"Well," I say, swinging her into my arms, "we have a lot to make up for."

I carry her to her couch, which is much more comfortable than my futon, and we tear off each other's clothes and make love. Then we put our costumes back on and dance like a meteorite is about to destroy life as we know it...and then we have sex in bed and eat a box of Christmas chocolates.

It is, without a doubt, the best Christmas ever.

Epilogue

Caitlin

"Finally!" Eugene exclaims when Wes and I show up at his New Year's Eve party.

"It's only eight-fifteen," Wes says. He's wearing a button-down blue shirt and jeans, plus a dorky NYE headband, and he looks pretty hot. "We aren't late."

"No, I mean, finally you two are together."

"Yes, *finally*," says another of our classmates from Waterloo. He walks over and slaps Wes on the back. "I knew you two would figure it out eventually."

Huh. Apparently everyone was expecting this except me.

See, you can be a CEO and still have some pretty big blind spots.

You can be the CEO of a company known for its popular dating app and still spend all of your twenties single or dating men who are totally wrong for you.

But now I'm thirty, and a new year is about to begin, and I've been decidedly *not* single for the past week. Wes and I have spent every night together—some at my house, some at his apartment—and it's been incredible.

My new boyfriend is perfect for me.

I'm only just starting to wrap my mind around the fact that this gorgeous man has loved me from afar for as long as we've known each other. The immensity of it, like the size of the dinosaurs, is still hard to grasp.

Although I'm an expert, of sorts, in finding love online, I found it the good old-fashioned way: I met a boy at school when I knocked him on his ass, and I proceeded to spend the next twelve years blind to how good we could be together, even as we stayed friends.

Now, I feel like I'm wrapped in the softest, warmest blanket, and it will always be there to protect me from the cold.

We haven't been together long, but we're building our relationship from a strong foundation—unlike our gingerbread house—and I know it will last.

Wes hands Eugene a key lime pie we bought at Happy as Pie. We'd planned to do some baking for the party, but we ended up spending all afternoon in bed. Funny how that happened.

Wes leads me to the kitchen, pours me a Coke and himself some alcoholic punch, and we clink our glasses together.

"I like your headband." He winks at me.

"I like yours, too."

"You used to wear headbands all the time in school. I remember that."

"I did, but a lot has changed in the past twelve years."

Not the way he feels about me, though. When I think of the man in my life, I'm positively giddy, which isn't something I usually feel.

We spend the party talking to new friends and old, but never leaving each other's sides. At midnight, Wes gives me the greatest kiss a woman could ask for.

"I love you," I whisper, "and I can't wait to go home and get you naked."

"I love you, too. Let's get out of here soon, okay?"

And that's how our new year together begins.

There's no doubt in my mind that it's going to be one very special year.

About the Author

Jackie Lau decided she wanted to be a writer when she was in grade two, sometime between writing "The Heart That Got Lost" and "The Land of Shapes." She later studied engineering and worked as a geophysicist before turning to writing romance novels. Jackie lives in Toronto with her husband, and despite living in Canada her whole life, she hates winter. When she's not writing, she enjoys gelato, gourmet donuts, cooking, hiking, and reading on the balcony when it's raining.

To learn more and sign up for her newsletter,
visit jackielaubooks.com.

Also by Jackie Lau

Love, Lies, and Cherry Pie

Time Loops & Meet Cutes

Donut Fall in Love Series
Donut Fall in Love
The Stand-Up Groomsman

Weddings with the Moks Series
Four Weddings to Fall in Love
Three Reasons to Run
Two Friends in Marriage

Chu's Restaurant Series
The Sitcom Star
The Reluctant Heartthrob

Kwan Sisters/Fong Brothers Series

Grumpy Fake Boyfriend

Mr. Hotshot CEO

Pregnant by the Playboy

Bidding for the Bachelor

Cider Bar Sisters Series

Her Big City Neighbor

His Grumpy Childhood Friend

Her Pretend Christmas Date (novella)

The Professor Next Door

Her Favorite Rebound

Her Unexpected Roommate

Holidays with the Wongs Series

A Match Made for Thanksgiving

A Second Chance Road Trip for Christmas

A Fake Girlfriend for Chinese New Year

A Big Surprise for Valentine's Day

Baldwin Village Series

One Bed for Christmas (prequel novella)

The Ultimate Pi Day Party

Ice Cream Lover

Man vs. Durian

Chin-Williams Series

Not Another Family Wedding

He's Not My Boyfriend